Confetti Girl

Confetti Girl

by Diana López

SCHOLASTIC INC.
New York Toronto London Auckland
Sydney Mexico City New Delhi Hong Kong

ISBN 978-0-545-23706-2

12 11 10 9   11 12 13 14 15/0

Printed in the U.S.A.   40

First Scholastic printing, March 2010

To Mom and Dad

CASCARONES

What are *cascarones*?
Festive, hollow eggshells, filled with confetti, that are cracked on people's heads, scattering confetti all over the place and bringing everyone good luck!

How to Make *Cascarones*

Step 1: Buy a dozen eggs.

Step 2: Carefully crack eggs at narrow tip, keeping most of the egg intact, and pour out the yolks and egg whites.

Step 3: Gently wash the eggshells.

Step 4: Soak eggshells in a bowl with 1 tablespoon white vinegar, ¾ cup hot water, and 4–5 drops food coloring.

Step 5: Buy confetti or make your own by hole-punching used magazines or newspapers.

Step 6: After the eggshells have dried, pour confetti into the eggshell.

Step 7: Cut out circles of tissue paper and glue over the hole.

Step 8: Quietly sneak up to people and . . . crack the confetti eggs on their heads!

27-Pound Egg

Some people collect coins or stamps, but I collect socks. I have a dresser with drawers labeled DAILY SOCKS, LONELY SOCKS, HOLEY SOCKS, and SOCK HEAVEN.

The daily drawer helps me get dressed every morning. When I'm bored, I reorganize it. I group the socks by color. Then I group them by style — dressy, casual, or athletic. Then by length — ankle, crew, or knee-high.

The lonely sock drawer is for those who have lost their partners. Most of the partners disappear in the washing machine or dryer. I can't explain it. Somewhere between the tossing and soaking and wringing, one gets lost. I don't know where it goes. Maybe aliens abduct it.

Holey socks aren't for angels. They actually have holes, so I don't wear them anymore. Sometimes, these socks become puppets and sometimes they go to sock heaven where they can rest in peace with the socks I've outgrown.

But mostly, I use the holey socks for experiments. People who think socks are just for feet have no imagination. For example, you can cover your ears with socks. Ankle socks make good earmuffs. Knee-highs are great for people who want to be rabbits or donkeys for Halloween. Then there's the sock rock. I've got a pile of these in a shoe box by my bed. I roll the sock and make a ball by folding the open end over the roll. Socks are also great as coasters, bookmarks, wallets, and dusters. There's no end to what they can do.

I admit that spending so much energy on socks is weird and a little immature, but it's hard to be normal when you live in a house with no TV. The reason I don't have a TV is because my dad's a high-school English teacher, which means he'd rather read. And because he's always reading, I got stuck with a stupid name, Apolonia Flores. The Flores part isn't so bad since it means "flowers" in Spanish. But Apolonia?

"What kind of name is that?" I ask my dad.

"It's the girl form of Apollo," he says. "He was the god of the sun. Get it? It's my way of calling you a sunflower."

"I'd rather be called Sun Flores. That's close enough, don't you think?"

But my dad doesn't hear me.

"According to the Greeks," he says, "the sun was the golden wheel of a chariot that Apollo drove across the sky. He was also the god of music, poetry, medicine, and fortune-telling."

Whenever my dad speaks, I can't help thinking that he looks like the teachers on Disney Channel specials — graying hair, lean body, wire-rimmed glasses. He always acts the part, even at home. It makes asking questions dangerous because something that takes most fathers five minutes to explain, takes mine an hour.

Thank goodness my name is too long, even for my father. Everybody calls me Lina instead. My dad says Lina sounds a lot like Leda, a girlfriend of Zeus, king of the gods. He disguised himself as a swan when he visited her, so now I'm named after someone who dated a bird.

Having an English teacher for a dad also means that instead of a dining room, we have a library, and instead of bedrooms, we have libraries, and we can probably call the kitchen a library too — even the pantry! — because next to my Pop-Tarts and Dad's *chicharrones* are books.

And they aren't in any order! The school librarian has the Dewey Decimal system, which makes finding books easy. But at my house, Dad's got *Be Your Own Handyman* next to *100 Favorite Love Poems* and *Birds of North America* next to *Tex-Mex Cooking*. So if I'm looking for a book on cats, I've got to read every title. This can take hours because Dad doesn't have a pattern when he stacks the books. Some titles read top to bottom while others read bottom up, and the titles of horizontal books are up-side down as often as they're right side up.

Anyone can see the books are used. All the paperback spines are creased, and the hardback jackets, torn. The pages are yellowed, dog-eared, underlined, highlighted, and tagged with pink or lime green Post-its. Other than that, the books are clean, which is weird because my dad will forget to dust the coffee table long before he forgets to dust his books. He stands before a shelf with a rag, pulls out the books one by one, and wipes the dust off. This eats up hours.

"Why don't you get rid of them?" I ask.

"Remember," he says, *"los amigos mejores son libros."*

This means that books are your best friends. In addition to quoting poetry, Dad likes to say *dichos,* Spanish proverbs. I'm not really bilingual, but I know that *el gato dormido no caza ratón* means "the sleeping cat doesn't catch the rat" and that *una acción buena enseña más que mil palabras* means "actions speak louder than words."

"Besides," Dad says, "I'm a bibliophile. *Biblio,* remember, is the Latin word for 'book,' and *phile* is the Greek word for 'lover.' Put them together and what do you have?"

"Book lover?"

"That's right."

"So does that make me a sockio-phile?" I ask.

One day, I tried counting my dad's books but gave up around 600. I tried again, giving up at 923. I thought I could get my dad's name into the book of *Guinness World Records*. I'd been reading it in the car every time Dad drove me to school or to volleyball games. I learned that the farthest human cannonball flight is 185 feet. If a football field is 300 feet, then imagine a guy flying over two-thirds of it. Wow! I also learned that the heaviest egg ever found was 27 pounds. More than two ten-pound bowling balls! It came from an elephant bird that went extinct a long time ago. I don't know who has the most books, but I did learn that the most books typed backward is 58. Now that's weird!

How can I *not* read when I live in a house with so many books? Sometimes I trip over one, pick it up, and before I can stop myself, I'm skimming the pages.

We have plenty of fairy tales and poems and big, fat books Dad calls epics, but I'm a facts-and-figures kind of girl. My favorite book is *Gray's Anatomy*. It's all about the human body. With my middle-school vocabulary, I can't really understand all the words, but the pictures are great, especially the transparencies, clear pages that show the layers of the body starting with the bones, then the heart and lungs, then the stomach and intestines, then the muscles. I can look at those pictures for hours.

Yes, *Gray's Anatomy* is a good book. It shows me how the body works. The only thing it can't tell me is how the body *doesn't* work. Believe me, I've looked. I've looked long and hard. Because I want to understand how my mom died last year. She was healthy, perfectly healthy, until she fell, cut her leg, and got a blood infection from something called staphylococcus. I didn't understand it, any of it, but I sure tried.

A few months after the funeral, I asked my dad, "What's a staphylococcus infection?"

"Well, *m'ija*," he said with his teacher's voice, "*staphylo* comes from the Greek word *staphulē*, which means 'a bunch of grapes.'"

"But that doesn't make any sense," I said. "Are you telling me a bunch of grapes hurt Mom?"

He didn't answer. For the first time, my dad didn't answer. He just put down his head and cried.

Egg Therapy

My dad started reading a lot more when my mom died. Sometimes when I dream about him, I see a body, a neck, and a book where his face should be.

"Are you okay?" I ask, peeking through his bedroom door.

"'O, that this too too solid flesh would melt,'" he says.

Sometimes I can't stand being in the house with my father so sad. Thank goodness Vanessa lives across the street. She's been my best friend since forever. We play volleyball together. We do our homework. We talk about clothes, global warming, and boys. *Ugly Betty* is our hero. Our rule at restaurants is to eat the one thing we've never tried even if it's *tripas,* a Tex-Mex dish made out of cow intestines.

We should be twins after all the time we spend together, and maybe we are twins, personality-wise. But in looks? Except for our brown hair and eyes, Vanessa and I are as different as a swan and an ostrich. She's the swan, and I'm the ostrich. I'm really the ostrich — the tallest girl in class, all legs. Too tall and skinny for my jeans no matter what size I buy. Everything is high water. That's why I'm a sockio-phile. I need something to hide my knobby ankles. Today my socks remind me of whitecaps on the ocean because they're aqua with white lace around the cuff.

Vanessa doesn't need a zillion socks. Everything fits perfectly — never too long or too short, too tight or too loose. And she never has a bad hair day. She could spend thirty minutes in front of a high-speed fan without getting tangles. If she wanted, she could make a paper sack look like something a model would wear.

I should be jealous, but I'm not. I don't care about my looks. I care more about volleyball, geometry, and how toasters and lawn mowers work. But, I admit, when Jason Quintanilla called me Daddy Longlegs, I went to the girls' restroom to cry. Not because I care what Jason thinks, even if he *is* the most popular boy in school, but because he called me Daddy Longlegs in front of Luís Mendoza, someone I *do* care about. Luís didn't laugh at the joke, but he didn't defend me either. He just stared at the sundial he wears on his wrist. I have such a big crush on him. How can I *not* like someone with a sundial instead of a normal watch? And he really can tell time when it's not rainy and cloudy, and that's almost always in Corpus Christi, Texas.

Of course, Vanessa knows all about my crush on Luís, since it's my favorite topic of conversation. And I know all about her crush on a guy named Carlos.

I decide to get out of my house and walk across the street to Vanessa's. When I see her mom through the front screen door, I tiptoe to the backyard.

"Hey, Vanessa," I call through her bedroom window.

She's on the phone. She says, "Can I call you back later? Lina's here — yes, I promise — ditto — you know I do. Do I have to say it?" She cups her hand over the receiver and whispers, "I love you, too." Then she hangs up.

"Who was that?" I ask as she holds open the screen so I can climb in.

"My dad. You came just in time to save me from apologizing to his girlfriend. I guess I hurt her feelings."

"How?"

"I called her a Windsor and then I told her what it means."

If that's true, then Vanessa told her dad's girlfriend that Windsor means more purses and shoes than brains. It's a word Vanessa and I made up. We use it when we're talking about stuck-up girls who think they really live in Windsor Castle.

Vanessa has two beanbags, one blue and the other red. I plop onto the blue one as if I own it, and in a strange way, I do. I didn't buy it and Vanessa never officially gave it to me, but the blue beanbag's mine — my little corner in her room. When she goes to *my* room, she hangs out on the top bunk.

"Why were you at my window?" Vanessa asks. "Is something wrong with my front door?"

I don't answer right away. How can I tell her I'm avoiding her mom? Especially when Ms. Cantu is such a wonderful woman? She's shown me so many grown-up things over the past year about washing clothes and cooking, things my mother was just starting to teach me. She even buys me girl stuff from the grocery store, Clearasil and Kotex, because I'm too embarrassed to remind my dad. I should be glad to see Ms. Cantu, but every time I *do* see her, she hugs me and calls me *pobrecita* and makes me feel like an orphan.

"I didn't want to bother your mom," I say to Vanessa. "She's been so busy."

"Tell me about it. Guess what I had for dinner last night."

"Eggs?"

"And for lunch today."

"More eggs?"

"That's right," Vanessa says. "How many times can you eat scrambled eggs without scrambling your brain?"

Around Easter, most people hard-boil eggs before painting them with dyes made by dissolving colored tablets in hot vinegar. But in Texas, we make *cascarones*, confetti eggs. Instead of hard-boiling eggs, we carefully crack open a small hole on the top and let the insides spill out. Then we wash and dye the eggshells. After they dry, we stuff them with confetti and glue a circle of tissue over the hole. On Easter morning, we run around and crack the eggs on each other's heads. Confetti gets everywhere. It's a lot of fun.

Everybody loves *cascarones* around Easter time, but Ms. Cantu has made them a yearlong event. That's why poor Vanessa lives with mountains of eggs. They're everywhere — eggshells stacked on the kitchen table, above the fridge, on the couch — some blue, orange, or pink, and some still white — and next to the eggs are circles of tissue paper and piles of magazines and newspapers because Ms. Cantu believes in making her own confetti with a hole puncher.

"If only eggs made us better at volleyball," I say. Vanessa and I play for our school, but our team isn't very good.

Vanessa laughs. "Maybe we'd win a few games."

"If that were true, I'd come over and eat eggs all the time."

"I'd feed them to the whole team."

"I don't know what's crazier," I say, "reading all day like my dad or making *cascarones* like your mom."

"She calls it 'therapy.' I guess she's upset because my dad has a girlfriend. I don't know what the big deal is. It's time to move on. My parents have been divorced for three years."

"Maybe your mom thought he'd come back."

"But she doesn't *want* him back. She's a man-hater. When she isn't making *cascarones,* she's watching tele-novelas or the Lifetime Channel. All the stories are about rotten men who cheat on their wives."

"Well, *my* dad's not rotten," I say.

"Neither is mine, but try telling *her* that." Vanessa grabs a heart-shaped pillow and hugs it. "How's your dad doing?" she asks.

"I don't know. He can't talk without quoting some book or saying some *dicho* that doesn't make sense."

"It can't be worse than a mom who keeps making *cascarones.* Easter was five months ago!"

"At least she's not saying her flesh is going to melt."

"At least you don't have to eat your dad's version of therapy."

"What are we going to do?" I ask. "Our parents are so miserable."

"Don't worry," Vanessa says. "We'll think of something."

Don't Put Your Eggs in One Basket

Baker is our middle school, a brick building in a neighborhood with street names like Casa Grande, Casa Linda, Casa de Palmas, and our street, Casa de Oro, which means "house of gold." I felt nervous about starting middle school, but then I realized I could sign up for sports. During recess in elementary school, I was always the first girl that got picked for teams. I got picked before most of the guys because I was just as tough and fast. So Vanessa and I signed up for volleyball on the first week of school. For now, we have to play on the B-team, but if we're good enough, we'll get to play on the A-team next year.

I have lucky socks for game days — white athletic socks with an appliqué of our mascot, a bronco. Unfortunately, it takes more than lucky socks to win a game.

Coach Luna doesn't know much about volleyball, since she's really a math teacher. The only reason she works with us is because all the *real* coaches help the football team. Sometimes I hate the football players. Who can blame me? They get everything — pep rallies, cheerleaders, their scores on the morning announcements. I guess I can understand since the football team qualified for district finals, while our volleyball team has lost more than half its games. That's what happens when you have a coach who can't tell the difference between a spike and a block.

"Okay, girls," Coach Luna says in the locker room. "I know Hamlin is first in district, but don't let that intimidate you. Losing a game doesn't make you a loser for life. You still have high school and college and careers ahead of you. That's the game that *really* matters — the game of life. So, even if you lose *every* inning . . ."

"You mean match," someone says.

"Yes, match. Even if you lose every match, you'll still be winners in my book."

She gives a thumbs-up and hurries us out of the locker room.

We've got time before the game, so we run laps around the gym, stretch, practice our serves, then do a setup-and-spike drill. I see my dad walk in during our warm-up. He settles on the bleachers and opens a book. Luís is here too. He comes to every game to work at the popcorn machine for student council. Every time I look at him, he's scooping popcorn into paper sacks or counting change.

Maybe he doesn't belong on the cover of a magazine like *J-14*, but I think he's cute. Picture small, black-framed glasses on a curly-haired hero from my dad's Greek mythology book. That's Luís.

A few football players walk in, Jason among them. They must have finished practice early because their hair is wet from the showers.

Vanessa glances at the bleachers to look for her mom or her dad. She doesn't have to tell me about her disappointment when she doesn't find them. I know because we're best friends, and best friends can read each other's minds.

Then the Hamlin girls arrive.

They look like racehorses, tall and sleek. Their arms are meaty, not skin and bones like mine, and they don't breathe but snort. They're more muscular than boys in football pads.

"Genetic wonders, every one," Vanessa says.

I can only nod in amazement. "Genetic wonders" are people who don't need to work at being athletic or smart or musical. They're just born with the right DNA.

The floor suddenly quakes as the Hamlin coach walks in. There's only one way to describe her — the human version of a monster truck.

"I heard their coach was in the '96 Olympics," Vanessa says.

"No way," I tell her. "And we got stuck with a math teacher?"

The Hamlin coach lines up her team and guides the

girls through Tae Bo kickboxing moves. They're punching and kicking the air, making us wonder if there's a combat version of volleyball we didn't know about.

Coach Luna decides to copy the pro. She claps her hands and makes us line up.

"Okay, girls," she says. "Time to get serious."

We do jumping jacks, toe touches, and windmills. It's embarrassing.

Finally the referee blows the whistle. Three minutes till game time. We huddle, and Coach Luna names the starters and says, "Remember the *true* game."

We put our hands in the center for a cheer. "One, two, three! Baker Broncos!"

Meanwhile, the Hamlin girls huddle too. Their monster-truck coach taps a clipboard and angrily points at them. Then they put *their* hands in the center.

"We're going to fry 'em!" their coach says.

"Yeah!"

"Roast 'em!"

"Yeah!"

"Devour 'em!"

"Yeah!"

And together they chant, "Hamlin! Hamlin! Rhymes with champion! Yeah!"

If volleyball were a mind game, they'd have us beat. It doesn't take much to make us feel like wimpy appetizers before a feast.

We take our places, mine by the net since I'm the tallest girl. We crouch slightly. We brush off our insecurities. We're ready, we tell ourselves. We forget everything Coach Luna told us about the schools and jobs of the *true* game. We don't care if we're in middle school. We want to win. Volleyball *does* matter.

Hamlin's server dribbles a few times, looks for our weak spot, then executes a beautiful overhand that lands with a boom. All we do is stand like statues because the serve's too fast and powerful. I'm surprised there isn't a crater where it hit the court. We're in big trouble. Only two of us can serve overhand, and half the time, those serves clip the net.

For Hamlin's second serve, we move toward the ball, all of us, colliding in the middle like marbles.

"Next time, call it!" one of my teammates says.

The third serve drills toward us again.

"Mine!" Vanessa calls. She digs deep, hurls herself to the floor, and bumps the ball inches before it hits the ground. It shoots straight up. Another girl sets it for me, and BAM! SPIKE! Right past the Hamlin girls! A perfect play. The ball's ours.

Goldie's our first server. She's not very athletic, but her serves are brutal. In fact, we call her our "secret weapon." She shakes her bangs from her eyes, and executes a gentle underhand serve that floats straight up, nearly hitting the roof. We can't tell whether the ball will land on our side or theirs. The Hamlin girls can't tell either. They squint at the bright lamps overhead, and the ball falls inches from the net — their side! They scramble, but too late. The point's ours. Like I said, a secret weapon. I feel a guilty joy when their coach stomps.

Goldie's serve is usually good for a few points, but like they say, we shouldn't put all our eggs in one basket because the Hamlin girls are quick studies. We fool them only once. The ball is theirs again.

For every point we make, they make three or four. It's a quick game. We take a five-minute break and switch sides for game two. I no longer have my back to Luís and my dad, but I don't have time to search them out because it's our serve and I'm up.

I can serve overhand — when I'm lucky.

"You can do it," Vanessa says, full of hope.

Yes, I can, I say to myself. *Querer es poder. Querer es poder.* These are words my dad has drilled into me. Basically, they mean if I think good thoughts, then good things will happen. Maybe I can't bore a crater like the Hamlin girls, but I *can* make a pothole. So I throw the ball, ready to drill it down, and drill it I do . . . right under the net.

I feel horrible when my teammates slump. Soon the Hamlin girls are five points ahead. We're not appetizers after all — we're grease stains. That's how bad we're doing.

When I glance at my dad for encouragement, I can't believe my eyes. He's reading! During the worst game of my life! How could he? If Mom were here — well — *she'd* watch the game and she'd make Dad watch the game too. I want to yell at him. I don't care who hears. But then I notice Luís, who *is* paying attention — to me.

Right in the middle of my volleyball game, I get paralyzed. I can't turn away from Luís because he's smiling as if proud. I don't think he understands volleyball at all. Maybe he thinks it's like miniature golf where the lowest score wins. Or maybe . . .

Maybe he likes me. I smile back at him and wave. Then SLAP! — the volleyball hits my face with enough force to knock me down.

I hear the audience laugh when Jason says, "Check out Daddy Longlegs. The taller they are, the harder they fall." He points at me and cracks up. I'm sure Luís is cracking up, too. Now I know why he was smiling — not because he felt proud but because I looked ridiculous. And now I know why the football players come to our games, not for moral support but for laughs.

I can't take it. I run off the court to hide in the locker room.

A few minutes later, my teammates walk in.

"We lost," they say. "Hamlin creamed us."

My dad waits for Vanessa and me outside the gym. It's autumn and the days are getting cooler and shorter. By the time we begin our walk, the sky is a grayish purple and the first stars are out.

We don't say much. I feel humiliated by the whole volleyball slap incident and Vanessa's feeling stood up by her parents. My dad usually likes the peace and quiet, but for some reason, he's feeling chatty tonight.

"Ah," he says in a dreamy voice, "nights like this remind me of that Robert Frost poem, 'Stopping by Woods on a Snowy Evening.'"

"It's not snowing, Dad. It never snows in Corpus Christi."

"Is that a sour mood I hear?"

Vanessa says, "Can you blame us, Mr. Flores? We got creamed."

"Don't be so hard on yourself," he says. "From what I hear, Hamlin makes worms' meat out of everyone."

"Worms' meat?" I ask. "What's that supposed to mean?"

"Mercutio. Before he died, he said, 'They have made worms' meat of me.' Get it? Because when you die, you become food for the worms."

"Who cares?" I say. "I don't even know who Mercutio is."

"He's from *Romeo and Juliet*. His name comes from the word 'mercurial.'"

Vanessa says, "You mean like mercury, the stuff in old thermometers?"

"That's it exactly. A person who's mercurial is a person whose emotions are constantly going up and down. Very unpredictable, just like the weather."

My dad never stops, I think to myself, getting angrier by the minute. Why does he have to turn *everything* — even a volleyball game! — into a vocabulary lesson?

"Guess what, Dad? I don't care about worms and mercury and thermometers. We lost our game. And then I got hit in the face. Why don't you define that?!"

"Someone hit you?" he says, surprised and protective-sounding.

"Not *someone*. The volleyball. But you wouldn't know, would you? You're too busy reading stupid books."

"Give him a break," Vanessa tells me. "At least your dad came to support us."

"You call that 'support'?" Then I turn to my dad and say, "You like make-believe people more than real ones. More than your own daughter!"

With that, I run home. I want to hide in my room and cry, but since I don't have the key, I sit on the hood of the car and wait. My dad and Vanessa are a few minutes behind, and I watch as he sees her safely home and accepts a dozen *cascarones* from Ms. Cantu. Then he crosses the street to our door. He knows I'm there, a few feet away. I can *feel* his eyes on me, but I don't look back.

"I won't take a book next time," he says. "I promise."

It's his apology, but I'm too mad to accept it. After a moment, my dad unlocks the door and goes in, leaving it open behind him. I keep waiting. I wait a long time. I don't go in till I get sleepy and cold.

Buñolero, ¡haz tus buñuelos! –
Buñuelo maker, make your buñuelos!;
in other words, mind your own business!

Cascarones for Sale

The next morning, I'm still upset about the volleyball game, so when I grab a pair of socks, I don't notice that they're slightly different shades of blue till I'm ringing Vanessa's doorbell. As I wait for someone to answer, I hear Ms. Cantu shouting. Vanessa opens the door, ignoring her mom. Then she gets her things, slams the door, and almost runs down the sidewalk.

"Wait," I say, rushing to catch up. "What's going on?"

"Nothing," she says.

"Is this about last night's volleyball game?"

"No. Maybe. Just leave it alone, okay?"

I know better than to bug her when she doesn't want to talk, so I change the subject.

"Why are you carrying that eight-pound bag of potatoes?" I ask.

"Homemaking," she says. "Mrs. Rumplestine asked us to find a partner. I hooked up with Carlos. I'm bringing potatoes and he's bringing cloth napkins."

"You're working with Carlos again?"

"Sure. Why not?"

"Vanessa, every time you work with Carlos something bizarre happens, and the bizarre thing is always your fault. Remember last month and your famous pot holder cake? The whole school heard about it."

Vanessa and Carlos had baked a double-layer cake for Mrs. Rumplestine's class. Carlos turned over the first layer to frost it. Then Vanessa took charge of the second layer. She got the pot holder mittens, grabbed both sides of the pan, flipped it, and somehow sandwiched the pot holder between the two cakes. The whole class cracked up.

"I was so embarrassed," she admits. "Carlos must think I'm silly. I can tell by the funny way he looks at me."

"That funny look is called love."

"No it isn't," she says, but I catch her wondering about it.

We've known Carlos for years and mostly ignored him. He still wears high-tops and basketball jerseys, his style since the third grade, but over the summer, he got really cute and more interesting, even though he acts the same. Only now, since he's so cute, we *notice* and we *listen* when he talks about the NBA or tries to reenact scenes from his favorite comedy shows.

"Back to the potatoes," I say. "What are they for?"

"Who knows? I guess we're going to make potato salad and learn how to fold napkins the fancy way."

We spend the rest of our walk inventing potato recipes. When we get to school, we go in separate directions. I won't see Vanessa till our third-period class, science. I bet Corpus Christi is the only city that teaches marine biology as part of a science class. That's the best thing about living by the sea.

Luckily, the first two classes fly by, and before I know it, I'm with Vanessa again.

"Guess what?" she says. "Luís and I passed notes in history."

"You did?" I try not to show it, but I'm jealous. She knows I like him, so why does she torture me?

"About you, dummy," she says. "Look."

She hands me a folded paper. I open it up. *Hi, Vanessa,* it says. *Sorry about last night's game. Is Lina okay?* Then I see Vanessa's handwriting. *Yes. Thanks for asking.* Then there's a smiley face with Luís's curly hair and glasses.

"That's it?" I say.

"It shows he cares."

"No it doesn't. It shows he saw the most embarrassing moment of my life."

"Shush!" she says, grabbing the letter. "Here he comes."

Luís walks in and sits sideways in the desk in front of me. I say hello, and he waves back. I ask how he's doing, and he nods and smiles as if to say "okay." That's it. The same routine every day. I don't have a chance. That note was about pity, not love.

"Okay," Mr. Star says. "For your semester project, you're going to do a five- to ten-minute presentation on some aspect of the Gulf Coast. And since most of you think the coast is only about fish, I've put some interesting topics on note cards."

He fans the cards, hiding the topics, and then he goes around the room and tells us to pick one. I get whooping cranes. Vanessa gets sand dune plant life. Carlos gets coastline trash. I ask Luís about his topic. He shows it to me — sand dune animal life. Others get oil rigs, sea turtles, brown pelicans, hurricanes, and barnacles.

"Hey, Luís," Carlos says after class. "Want to trade topics?"

"Sure," Luís says.

"Did you hear that?" Vanessa whispers. "Looks like Carlos wants to work with sand dunes, too. I guess we'll be doing two projects together."

After science, Vanessa and I go to English class. Mrs. Huerta likes her students in alphabetical order, so we don't get to sit together. Lately I've been sleepy in English. Fourth period is the most boring hour of my day.

Near the end of class, Mrs. Huerta says, "We're starting a new book, *Watership Down*." She hands out copies of a paperback with a picture of a rabbit on the cover. "Read the first four chapters tonight," she says as we walk out.

I practically sleep through my afternoon classes. Soon the final bell rings. Laughter and slamming locker doors echo through the hallways. In ten minutes, the building clears except for the "Hollywoods" of the school, the stars of the Baker Show. Every school has them — a handful of students that go for the extracurricular activities or make the honor roll or act like class clowns. Everyone else is a "Hollywood extra" — nameless, faceless, background noise, sofa slugs at home.

Dr. Rodriguez, the principal, has asked all club officers to help plan the annual Halloween carnival, so I head to the cafeteria. Vanessa and I are the captains of girls' athletics. The position was offered to the older girls first, but none of them wanted to deal with the extra work. I guess the same thing happened with the guys since Jason's the captain of boys' athletics.

When I walk in, I see a couple of Windsors from the pep squad and all the smart honors kids or "eggheads."

I take a seat as far from Jason as possible, but he sees me anyway.

"So what's it like to spike a volleyball with your face?" he says. Everyone laughs. All I can do is sink in my chair, but I'm too tall to hide.

A few seconds later, Luís, who is the student council

treasurer, enters, looks around, and sits beside me. Love or convenience?

When Vanessa walks in, everyone starts laughing again. Her eight-pound bag of potatoes is wearing a diaper!

"Teen pregger!" Jason says, and a few others join in.

Fortunately, she's not alone. Some other students, including a boy, come in with potato babies, too.

"Can you believe it?" she says, taking the seat across from Luís and me. "Mrs. Rumplestine wants us to treat the potato bag like a baby. She says eight pounds is the average weight of an infant. It doesn't sound like much, but try carrying it around for an hour."

"And Carlos is the father?" I tease.

She blushes when she nods a yes.

Luís says, "Is i-i-i-it a-a boy or a girl?"

Because he's usually so quiet, I forget that he gets stuck on a syllable sometimes, most of the time. Then when he gets past the hard part, the rest of his words come fast, too fast. So he's embarrassed to talk, especially around bullies. But Vanessa and I, and a few other enlightened people, don't care.

"A girl," Vanessa says. "Her name's Duchess."

"Duchess?" I can't help laughing. "Does Carlos know that his 'daughter' is named after your dead dog?"

Luís shakes with the giggles.

"No," Vanessa says. "As far as he's concerned, she's royalty."

Dr. Rodriguez walks in and starts the meeting. I like her. She's tall like me and has a no-nonsense discipline style. Miss Luna should take lessons.

"We need to sign up for booths," Dr. Rodriguez says. "I'll give you a few minutes to brainstorm. Then we'll make a list. If two groups want the same booth, we'll flip a coin to see who gets it. No food booths, please. Your teachers will be selling the refreshments because they have food-handling certificates. Any questions?"

She answers a few while Vanessa and I list our top three choices: the jail, the Coke bottle ring toss, and the face-painting booth. When it's time to regroup, we discover that we've tied for them all! To make matters worse, we lose the coin flip every time. I should have worn my lucky socks today.

"What are we going to do?" I say. "I'm all out of ideas."

Whenever Vanessa needs to problem solve, she looks up and touches her chin. When I look up, all I see is the ceiling or the sky or the roof of the car, but when Vanessa looks up, she sees answers.

After a second or two, she waves her hand to get Dr. Rodriguez's attention. "Girls' athletics," she announces, "will sell *cascarones*. Dozens and dozens of *cascarones*."

Dr. Rodriguez raises a curious eyebrow, then writes "Cascarones Booth" by our names.

"That's a great idea," I tell Vanessa.

"Just killing two birds with one stone — raising money *and* getting rid of all those eggs."

"It's perfect."

She puts a reassuring hand on my shoulder. "Don't worry, Lina. For our next fundraiser, we're having a book sale."

Another genius plan. It's great having a brainiac for a best friend.

Vinegar Stinks Up the House

On the walk home, Vanessa says, "Will you carry Duchess for a while?"

She hands me her potato baby, and I take hold right above the twisty.

"Not like that!" she says. "You're swinging her by the hair. You've probably disconnected her neck or something."

"It's a bag of potatoes, Vanessa."

"That bag of potatoes is my homemaking project, and I plan to get an A." She carefully takes the "baby" from me. "Now make a cradle with your arms," she says.

I make a cradle, and she gently places the baby there.

It's a lumpy thing, and since the potatoes are in a mesh bag, dirt gets on my arms.

"Your baby needs a bath," I tease, but she ignores me.

We get to her house and enter through the kitchen door.

"It's me," Vanessa calls to her mom in the other room.

Then she runs to the restroom, and while she's gone, I hide the potato baby in the fridge. She comes back and searches all over the kitchen, begging for clues.

"Lina!" she scolds when she finds Duchess. "Babies *die* in the cold." She grabs the baby and holds it against her chest as if to warm it. "Wait till I get my hands on *your* next project," she says.

Vanessa's only pretend-mad. First chance I get, I'm going to kidnap her baby and send a ransom note for ten bucks. I might even put a French fry in the envelope the way real kidnappers put thumbs, little tocs, or ears to show they're serious.

"Let's go tell my mom about the carnival," Vanessa says. She wraps the potato baby in a towel and carefully puts it on the table. I guess Duchess is asleep. Apparently, leaving a baby on the kitchen table is not as bad as carrying it by the hair. As soon as Vanessa's satisfied, we head to the living room, where her mom's watching TV.

Ms. Cantu always gets home before we do. She used to be a stay-at-home mom, but after her divorce, she became the odd-job queen. She's a part-time office assistant at Ray High School, where my dad teaches. She sells Avon. And two or three times a month, people rent her decorations and hire her to set up dance halls for their weddings or *quinceañeras*.

Because of her decorating business, Ms. Cantu's garage is packed with candelabras, vases, ruffled table skirts, and a huge heart-shaped *arco*. There's also a giant birdcage for Romeo and Juliet, her doves. When they're not cooing at weddings, they stay in a smaller cage in the living room.

Ms. Cantu doesn't put much effort into her decorating business. She says it breaks her heart to see brides and grooms when she knows about the fifty-percent divorce rate. The only reason she gets jobs is because she doesn't charge much, which is also the reason she never gets to decorate the fancy rooms at Selena Convention Center where the *real* dances are. Most of the weddings and *quinceañeras* she decorates take place at Tito's Icehouse or Milagros Dance Hall, an old barn off Robstown Road.

"Hi, Mom," Vanessa says.

"Hi, *m'ija*." Ms. Cantu spots me standing by the kitchen doorway. "Ay, Lina. Don't be so shy. Come here." She pats the sofa cushion and I obediently sit beside her. "*Pobrecita*, Lina. Growing up without a mama. And she was such a good woman. My closest friend."

She hugs me and pats my back as if burping a baby. I have to stoop since I'm so tall.

"That's enough, Mom," Vanessa says. "You're smothering her."

Ms. Cantu lets me go. "I can't help it," she says, almost in tears. "I can't stand a real-life tragedy. And your father is such a good man, Lina. He doesn't deserve this."

I want to say that my father isn't as good as she believes, that he can be selfish like all other men, that he'd rather read books than pay attention to his poor orphan daughter.

"Come help me with these *cascarones,* girls."

Vanessa and I sit around the coffee table. Ms. Cantu has already dyed the eggs, using bright colors like yellow, hot pink, and red. She's also painted stripes or flowers on the shells. The whole house stinks like vinegar. While Vanessa cuts out circles of tissue paper, I grab a handful of confetti and carefully pour it into the shell. Then I hand it to Ms. Cantu, so she can glue tissue over the hole.

"So what are you watching?" Vanessa asks.

"A show on Lifetime, *Heart of Sacrifice.*"

"What's it about?"

"This woman falls in love with a man, and he loves her too, and everything's perfect until she finds out he's married. So now he's trying to sweet-talk her into being his woman on the side. Can you believe it? And that *tonta*'s falling for it."

"Didn't you see that movie last week?" Vanessa asks.

"No."

"Yes, you did. On the Spanish station."

"No, no, that was *Dos Amores, Una Vida.*"

"Two loves, one life?" I ask.

"Yes. And it was a completely different story. In that one, the man loved two women, really loved them, and he couldn't pick between them, so one of the women takes matters into her own hands and murders the competition."

"And he marries the murderer?" Vanessa guesses.

"*¿Quién sabe?* It's not over yet. It's got two weeks to go. But my guess is that he's going to fall for her sister. That's how it is with men. They think forever means three weeks. Just look at your father."

Ms. Cantu always puts down her ex-husband. Vanessa's shoulders slump, so I decide to change the subject.

"Did you decorate that shirt?" I ask, pointing to Ms. Cantu's big T-shirt with buttons in the center of appliquéd flowers. All her shirts are crafty. That's her style. She wears old-fashioned stirrup pants with tennis shoes or sandals and oversized T-shirts decorated with iron-on transfers, fabric paint, sequins, buttons, lace, and bows.

"You like it?" she says, straightening her shirt to give us a better look.

"Yeah. Where did you get those buttons?"

"These?" She points to them. "I plucked them off my ex-husband's coat."

"The black one?" Vanessa says.

"Yup."

"Dad *loves* that coat. He's been looking for it."

"He should have looked before leaving me."

"But that's cruel, Mom. How could you destroy his favorite coat?"

"I didn't destroy it. I just found a better use for it."
Ms. Cantu turns to me. "The buttons are made of wood,
see? Very easy to paint. That's how I got these bright
colors."

"If you ask me," Vanessa says, "it's an ugly shirt.
And I'm not talking about the decorations, even if it's *just
plain wrong* to steal buttons. I'm talking about the shape.
Why are your shirts extra large when you're small enough
for a medium? You could wear real cute clothes if you
wanted."

"I need big T-shirts," Ms. Cantu says, "so I can have
room for my iron-ons."

"But you have a nice figure. Why hide it? How's a
sweet guy going to notice you? Especially when you wear
socks with your sandals."

"Socks are cool," I say.

"With sandals, Lina?"

As much as I hate to dis socks, I have to agree. There
is a high tacky index for wearing them with sandals.

"I'm just saying you're a babe, Mom. You should
show off your babehood."

"What for?" Ms. Cantu says, grabbing a purple
Sharpie and scribbling on the eggs. "Here's my answer
next time some man asks me on a date." She writes "as
if" on the first egg. "You wish," on the second. Then,
"when pigs fly," "talk to the hand," and "I'd rather eat
worms." The marker ink smears until the eggs get a
blotched look.

"You're ruining them," Vanessa complains.

We don't say anything for a while. The woman on *Heart of Sacrifice* is packing her bags and leaving her boyfriend. Good for her. She wants to be *more* than the woman on the side. She wants to be the main character in her man's life — the protagonist, my dad would say. And why shouldn't she be? I wouldn't mind ousting the hero of my dad's favorite book and taking his place.

"Okay, let's talk about some good news," Vanessa says. "We're having a school carnival for Halloween and girls' athletics is in charge of a booth."

Ms. Cantu is quick to respond. "Oh, no! I'm not volunteering my face so people can throw pies at it."

"I wasn't asking you to."

"And I'm not sitting in the dunking booth, either."

"Let me finish, Mom."

Ms. Cantu eyes her suspiciously, then nods an okay.

"We're going to sell your *cascarones*," Vanessa announces.

I thought Ms. Cantu would holler and scream and punch the sky, but the exact opposite happens. She gets very quiet and looks off with a dreamy twinkle in her eye.

"That's genius!" she suddenly blurts. "We can use the carnival to test the market. Who says *cascarones* should be limited to Easter? We should make them a year-round commodity!"

"No, Mom," Vanessa says. "We're getting rid of them once and for all. It's embarrassing to live in a house that looks like a confetti-egg factory."

"Factory, yes. Another great idea." Ms. Cantu forgets us and starts talking to herself. "And I can use different themes. Orange and black dyes for Halloween. Red and green for Christmas. And for Thanksgiving . . . I can glue little beaks . . . or turkey feathers!"

Ms. Cantu heads for the kitchen, still brainstorming aloud.

"And I can have specialty confetti too," she says to herself. "Rice instead of paper for . . . for . . . yes . . . *wedding cascarones*!"

"Mom. Mom!"

Ms. Cantu doesn't hear her.

"I can't stand this!" Vanessa says. "I was trying to solve a problem, but instead I created a new one."

> *Una acción buena enseña más que mil palabras –*
> *Actions speak louder than words*

Papas con Huevos

Mom always had after-school projects waiting for me. "Can you help decorate cookies?" she'd say. Or, "Go outside and pick some flowers." Or, "Fix my nails, please." She loved to paint them, but since she wasn't co-ordinated with her left hand, her right-hand nails looked like a preschooler's coloring page.

I guess these projects were chores, but they were fun, too. Now when I come home, I've got to sweep, fold towels, or scrub the bathroom sink. Dad helps, but sometimes he makes a big mess.

Like today. He's got flour, potato skins, and crumpled napkins on the counter. The pot boils over with brown scum. And I don't want to talk to him because I'm still mad about the volleyball game, but I have to know what he's up to.

"What are you doing, Dad?"

"Making dinner. Thought I'd give you a break."

Except for game nights, dinner's my responsibility. I cook while Dad cleans — that's our rule. And even though I don't cook as well as Mom did, Dad never complains.

"What are you trying to make?" I ask.

"*Carne guisada* and *papas fritas*."

"You need a recipe for that?"

"Are you kidding? I need a recipe for peanut butter sandwiches."

How mad can a girl be at a man who makes fun of himself and wears a green frog apron that says KISS THE COOK and tube socks over his hands for potholders?

We clear space on the table. Dinner's served. The beef's tough and the *papas* are mushy, but who cares? I pretend it's delicious because my dad lets me blabber about the Halloween carnival. He laughs out loud when I describe Vanessa's potato baby and Ms. Cantu's creative *cascarones,* so I don't complain when I notice he served ranch-style beans straight from the can instead of heating them up first.

Everything's great until he asks about my English class.

"Any new vocabulary words?" he wants to know.

"I guess. Maybe. Super . . . super . . . super something. Can't remember."

"Was it *supersede*?" he asks. "*Supercilious? Super-fluous?*"

"I don't remember, Dad. It could have been *super-duper* or *super-loop* for all I care."

He gets sarcasm from his students all the time so he's good at ignoring it.

"Remember that *super* is a prefix that means 'above and beyond,'" he says. "So no matter what the word is, you can get its meaning if you take it apart."

"Okay, Dad. I get it. So did I tell you we're having a book sale for our next fundraiser?"

"What else are you doing in English?" he asks. "Reading any novels?"

I sigh, bored, but he doesn't get the hint. He just waits for my answer. "Yes," I finally say. "I don't remember the title, but it's got a rabbit on the cover."

"Is it *Watership Down*? It's got to be *Watership Down*."

"Yes, that's it. But I left it in my locker. I guess I can't do my homework."

"Nonsense. I've got a copy somewhere. Let me look."

He leaves the table to scan the bookshelves, and all of the sudden, I *care* about the tough beef, the mushy potatoes, and the cold beans. Why should I eat when my own father has abandoned his food? Nothing's more important than his books and vocabulary words. He might *say* I matter, but when he goes on a scavenger hunt for a book, I realize that I really don't.

I take my plate to the kitchen, grab my half-finished

soda, and head to my room. When I walk past him, he's kneeling to search the lower shelves. He's got a paper towel and wipes it lovingly over the titles as if polishing a sports car. He doesn't hear my angry, stomping footsteps. I catch the last part of his sentence.

". . . a classic epic journey," he says as if he were in class with a bunch of students. I can't stand it. I just can't stand it. I'd rather have Vanessa's crazy mom.

Later, just as I write *I love Luís* for the three-hundredth time, my dad peeks through my bedroom door.

"Found my copy of *Watership Down,*" he says, handing me a paperback whose spine's been taped a dozen times. "How far do you have to read tonight?"

"The first four chapters," I say.

"That's a lot. You better get busy."

"Sure, Dad. I'll start reading right away."

But I don't. As soon as he leaves, I put the book on my nightstand and use it as a coaster. The condensation from my soda makes a big, wet circle on the cover.

The next morning, Vanessa knocks on my door. She holds out her potato baby.

"Did Duchess lose weight?" I ask.

"Is it *that* obvious?"

I nod. "What happened?"

"*Dinner* happened. Guess what I ate last night?"

"Eggs?"

"That's a given. What *kind* of eggs?"

"Don't tell me," I say. "You ate *papas con huevos*!"

"That's right. Remember how I left Duchess on the kitchen table? Well, part of her got peeled, diced, and fried. I didn't realize I was eating my own daughter till halfway through my second *taquito*!"

"You're a cannibal," I tease.

"It's all my mom's fault. Just like everything else in my life."

"Don't blame your mom when you left the potatoes on the table. Of course she used them."

"I guess you're right," Vanessa says. "So, can I borrow some potatoes to fatten her up?"

"Sure," I tell her. "No problem." But it *is* a problem because I look in the fridge and see that Dad used all our potatoes last night.

"What do I do now?" Vanessa cries. "I can't let Carlos know that I put Duchess in danger. We'll get an F and he'll never talk to me again."

Usually, she looks at the ceiling and touches her chin for the answer. But not today. I've never seen her so stressed. I've got to calm her down before she pulls out a clump of hair and goes bald. I make her sit and serve her a glass of water. Then I go to the backyard and search for potato-size rocks, finding four near the fence. With a little reshuffling, we manage to hide them in the potato bag. Duchess is as good as new.

"You're a genius," Vanessa says. "I don't know what I'd do without you."

I take a bow. "Best friend, at your service."

Scrambled Eggs for Brains

A week later, we have our last volleyball game. Our team didn't make it for district finals. Big surprise. But we've got one more game, and we're going to finish with dignity.

"Because," Coach Luna tells us in the locker room, "sometimes you win, sometimes you lose, but never, ever, *ever* do you quit. Besides, the A-team coach promised to watch. She wants to recruit players for her team."

With that, she sends us to the gym to warm up. My dad's already there. He waves and does a little mime to say, "Look! NO BOOKS!" I give him a happy thumbs-up to show my approval. Then Ms. Cantu enters the gym. She walks straight onto the court, magically dodging stray balls.

"I'm wearing a special game shirt for you," she tells Vanessa. It's a red extra-large T-shirt. She sewed on a big, felt volleyball, painted Vanessa's number on it, and randomly glued a few stars. It's tacky but sweet. "I'm here for support," she adds, "but if your dad shows up with that girlfriend of his, I'm leaving." With that, she does an about-face and heads to the bleachers, spotting my dad and taking the seat beside him.

Ms. Cantu and my dad get along okay. All their conversations are about Vanessa and me — and sometimes my mom. I doubt they have real heart-to-hearts, but they're close enough to call each other by their first names — Irma, pronounced "ear-ma" with a little roll on the *r* — and Homero, also pronounced with a little *r*-roll.

This time we're playing against Tom Brown Middle School. I'm not really nervous about losing, even though it's a real possibility. I'm more nervous about playing in front of the A-team coach. I *really* want to make a good impression. Maybe I can get permission to practice with the A-team during the off-season. I hear they sometimes work with B-team players who show a lot of potential.

When the game starts, I dive for balls and risk more volleyball slaps when I block the spikes. We win one. Tom Brown wins one. So we get the third tie-breaking game. It's close. The serve goes back and forth. We're never more than two points apart. I'm doing my best, really shining, because the A-team coach is taking notes and my dad's here without a book. Vanessa's doing her best too because her mom's actually taking a break from *cascarones* and telenovelas. In fact, I'm too focused on my game to notice that Luís isn't at the popcorn machine. When I *do* notice, I figure he's in the bleachers, do a quick scan, and realize I'll never spot him because *everyone's* here — all the teachers that have been promising to come and lots and lots of students.

Their energy *feeds* us. We're hyped. We've got the hopes of all our friends, teachers, and parents on our shoulders, and we don't want to disappoint.

Amazingly, we win. Coach Luna jumps up and down, cheering, and giving all of us high fives.

After getting my things from the locker room, I find my dad.

"Lina," he says, waving me over, "I was just talking to Mrs. Hammett."

She's the A-team coach, a *real* coach with tennis shoes and polyester shorts.

"It's a pleasure to meet you," she says. "I was just telling your dad that you should join the A-team at volleyball camp next summer."

"Really?" I can't hide my excitement.

"Here's a brochure," Mrs. Hammett says. "There's a good camp at the University of Texas in San Antonio every summer. You'll get to stay in the dorms for two weeks, and you'll meet girls from all over Texas."

"Can I go, Dad?"

"As long as you keep up your grades."

"Oh, I will. I promise," I say. "Can I have an extra

brochure, Mrs. Hammett? I'd like to give one to my best friend, Vanessa."

"Sure," Mrs. Hammett says. "Here are a few extra. Pass them along."

We thank her, and she leaves to speak to the Tom Brown coach.

"Look what I have," I say when I find Vanessa and her mom in the parking lot outside the gym. "It's information about a volleyball camp next summer."

I hand the brochure to Vanessa.

"This looks like fun," she says. "Can I go, Mom?"

"Only if your dad's footing the bill. Money doesn't grow on trees, you know. At least not on *my* trees."

The next morning, Dr. Rodriguez announces our volleyball win over the intercom. Since Goldie and I are in Miss Luna's first-period class, she makes everyone applaud. I feel like a *real* Hollywood until I see Jason crossing his arms instead of clapping.

"Just because you won one stupid game," he says, "doesn't mean you're in the Olympics."

"Chill out," I say. "No one disses the football team because they get pep rallies and cheerleaders and candy bags in their lockers on game days."

"That's right," Goldie adds. "It can't be *all Jason all the time.*"

Even with Jason in the room, I enjoy math. My answers are right or they're wrong, no gray area, no guessing games. This week we've been learning how to calculate distance, and Miss Luna wants us to write a word problem using the equation "distance equals rate times time." I decide to add a few colorful details to mine.

After everyone stops scribbling, Miss Luna asks us to share our word problems.

One of my classmates says, "If a blue car travels eleven miles per hour for two hours, how far has it gone?"

"Twenty-two miles," we all answer.

"If a red car," the next person says, "travels twenty miles per hour for three hours, how far has it gone?"

"Sixty miles."

"If a green car . . ."

"I can't take this anymore," I say. "Did *everyone* write about cars?"

"Not me," Goldie says. "I wrote about a bowling ball."

"Let's hear your word problem then," Miss Luna says.

"If a bowling ball travels ten feet per second for three seconds, how many feet has it gone?"

"Thirty feet," we all answer.

I love Goldie, but her bowling ball problem is just like everyone's car problem.

Finally, it's my turn. I stand up and clear my throat.

"A football player named Jason stuffs his face with three hot dogs before the game and gets severe stomach cramps during the second quarter. At the rate of five yards a second, he runs forty yards before he has to throw up. How long does it take for him to reach his upchuck zone?"

The whole class cracks up and I take a bow. But Jason isn't amused. When class ends, he "accidentally" bumps into me.

"So," he says, "can you *really* bend your knees backward?"

"What's *that* supposed to mean?"

"Whoop! Whoop!" he says, urging his friends to join him.

"What's wrong with you? You're acting like retards."

"Whoop! Whoop!" they say again.

"I think he's making fun of your science topic," Goldie says.

"What do whooping cranes have to do with anything?"

"They're tall," Jason explains, "ridiculously and uselessly tall!" He and his friends walk off, laughing harder than tickled babies. When they reach the end of the hall, I hear the "Whoop! Whoop!" again. Last month, I was a daddy longlegs spider; this month, I'm a bird, a ridiculously tall bird.

"How'd he find out about my science topic?" I ask Goldie. "He isn't even in my class."

"I don't know," she says.

I stomp to the restroom and grab a bunch of paper towels. Shredding them doesn't solve any problems, but it sure helps me deal with my anger.

When I get to Mr. Star's room, I see a chart with our names and projects. There are other charts, too, for other classes. Jason's class is studying animal family structures. He gets to do a report on lions. How do you make fun of lions? And why do whooping cranes have to be so tall?

"Hi, Vanessa," I say when she comes in.

She waves, but instead of coming to her desk, she goes to see Carlos. She's been talking to him a lot lately, and sometimes she doesn't notice I'm around.

Lucky for me, Luís comes in too. He sits in front of me and claps his hands.

"What's that for?" I ask.

"The g-g-game. I heard the announcements."

"Oh, thanks," I say. Then I realize he didn't know about our win until this morning. "Why didn't you go?"

"You see, I was uh, uh, trying out for the Christmas concert."

"That's great," I answer, thinking that a boyfriend who played an electric guitar or the drums would be cool. "What instrument do you play?"

He shakes his head.

"You don't play an instrument?"

He nods.

"So you're going to be part of the stage crew?" I say. "That sounds like fun. You get to design stage sets and work the spotlight and control the curtains."

He shakes his head again. He's about to speak, but I can't help babbling.

"You didn't make it?" I say. "Well, if you ask me, they're the ones missing out. Like I said, you'd be great at stage design. It takes a real artist for that."

He looks at his feet. His glasses slip down his nose. His curls fall forward.

"What's wrong?" I ask.

"You don't get it."

He sounds seriously mad — mad enough to forget stuttering. He takes one look at me, shakes his head, and turns away. He's right. I don't get it. What did I do wrong?

The bell rings, and Mr. Star says, "Vanessa, Carlos, get to your seats now."

I hear her settle in behind me. I should tease her about Carlos, but I'm too preoccupied by Luís. I take out a sheet of paper and write a note.

So what did you try out for? I ask. I fold it into a neat paper football and wait for Mr. Star to turn his back before passing it forward.

Luís slowly unfolds it. Then he bends forward to read it. A long time passes before he crumples it up. He keeps it in his hand, his fist tight around it. After another long time, he opens it up again and writes something back. His pencil's loud. I imagine him scraping his desk. He crumples the letter again and tosses it over his shoulder. It hits me on the chin and falls on my lap.

I open it, not knowing what to expect, and there's my answer, in all caps and with lots of exclamation points.

I TRIED OUT FOR CHOIR, YOU DUMMY!!!!!!!!

I've really got scrambled eggs for brains sometimes.

Cascarones War

Now that it's Halloween, I can't wait to show Vanessa my costume. We don't go for the cheap, polyester, one-size-fits-all costumes at Party City or for the expensive rentals at Starlight Ball where the outfits are good enough for Harry Potter movies . . . or *real* aliens. No, Vanessa and I believe in the homemade stuff. So I put on my red warm-ups and red slipper socks. I hide my hair in a red knit cap. I paint my face red and drape artificial ivy over my shoulders. And I've got my sign with pictures of fish, black X's over their eyes, and tombstones with S.I.P. for "Sink in Peace." Mom would have been proud. She'd say the costume is perfect and totally me and that no one else could have imagined such a unique idea. And, she would've guessed what I was, no problem. But my dad is clueless.

"So what are you?" he says. "No, no. Let me guess."

I turn around. Then I turn around again. I can't believe it's taking him so long to figure it out.

"Oh, I get it," he says. "You're a fish devil."

I'm too shocked by his ignorance to speak. I'm about to explain my *real* identity when the phone rings.

"We're ready," Vanessa says.

My dad and I walk across the street. As soon as Vanessa sees me, she says, "That is so totally cool, Lina! You're like Nemo's version of Satan."

I can't believe it. Even Vanessa gets it wrong, and *she's in my science class*!

Ms. Cantu comes to the door. She's got on a black T-shirt with a huge, happy-face pumpkin. She turns around. On the backside, the pumpkin face makes Freddy Krueger look like a teddy bear.

As soon as she finishes modeling, she twirls her finger and says, "Now it's your turn, Lina."

I turn around.

She's a little confused at first, but then she gets this glimmer in her eye. "*¡Qué chula!*" she says.

"Mom!" Vanessa says. "Lina's not trying to be cute. She's trying to be evil and sinister. She's a fish devil. Get it?"

"Fish devil?"

"Sure, what did you think she was?"

Could it be? Is Ms. Cantu the only one who understands my costume? Who actually *gets* me?

"I thought she was shrimp sauce," she says.

"Shrimp sauce?!"

We crack up. All of us. All at once. I give up. No one will ever get my costume.

After we get over the giggles, we load the truck with boxes and boxes of *cascarones* for the Halloween carnival. Ms. Cantu has made special eggs for the event. Using a white crayon, she drew different pumpkin faces on the shells. Then she dyed them orange. The wax from the crayon keeps the dye from sticking, so the eggs look like miniature pumpkin heads.

Every now and then, Vanessa stops to re-stuff herself. She's dressed as a scarecrow. She's wearing one of her father's flannel shirts and torn-up jeans. For hay, she's used *ojas*, corn shucks for steaming tamales. She's got them sticking out from her collar and cuffs and between the shirt buttons. She's also glued them along the inner rim of a cowboy hat. I think she's done a good job of making her hair look like hay.

The carnival is held in the school cafeteria and the courtyard. Goldie and some of the other girls have already decorated our booth with streamers and cutouts of pumpkins, black cats, witches, and ghosts. The sign says, CASCARONES: 20 CENTS EACH OR $1.50 A DOZEN. My dad and Ms. Cantu are the adult chaperones so they'll stay at the booth all night. The rest of us will take turns. Vanessa and I take the first shift.

A few people walk by, see the *cascarones,* and move on.

"I don't know," Vanessa says. "Maybe this was a bad idea."

"Are you upset about losing money or having to take the eggs back home?"

"Losing money *and* taking back the eggs," she says.

Eventually someone stops at the booth — Sum Wong, who likes to be called Sammy. I've known Sammy since the fourth grade.

"I like your fish devil costume," he says.

"I'm not . . ."

"So what's with these eggs?" he interrupts. "Is this some kind of Latino thing?"

"Yeah," Vanessa says. "You're supposed to sneak up on people and crack the eggs on their heads. All this confetti comes out. It's lots of fun."

"Really?" He raises an interested eyebrow, then reaches in his pocket for some money. He spends a long time staring at the carton, finally picking an egg with an evil-looking expression. He walks straight to a pep squad girl in front of the *taquito* booth and *CRACK!* breaks the eggshell on her head.

She shakes off the confetti. "Sammy!" she yells as he runs to hide. "I'm going to get you!" She marches to our booth, pays for an egg, and runs off. A few minutes later,

Sammy comes back for a dozen more. Before we know it, we've got a line. It's a *cascarones* war out there.

"This is wonderful!" Ms. Cantu says. "This proves my theory. *Cascarones* are fun *all year long*!"

My shift is almost over when a guy from my history class, Jorge, walks up. He's dressed as a policeman.

"Sorry, Lina," he says. "But I've got a warrant for your arrest."

"I can't go to jail," I say. "I was just getting ready to start enjoying the carnival."

"Rules are rules," he says.

"Go on," Vanessa says, "I'll get you out as soon as I'm finished here."

What a bummer, I think, but Jorge is right — rules are rules — someone paid fifty cents to put me in jail and someone else has to pay fifty cents to get me out.

The jail booth is outside in the courtyard. It has bars over the window, two benches, and a guard dressed as a mariachi. There's one prisoner, Sammy Wong.

"I guess the pep squad girls got tired of getting confetti out of their hair," he explains.

I take a seat to wait for Vanessa. Five minutes go by, nothing. Ten minutes, nothing. Where is she? Aren't friends supposed to look out for each other? When one of Sammy's friends pays his bail, I get more impatient.

"Okay, Lina," Jorge finally says. "You're free to go now. That guy over there paid your bail."

He points across the courtyard where Luís is leaning

against the tree. He's holding a headless Superman piñata. He's wearing a neon green T-shirt with a bright yellow "K."

I'm a little nervous when I approach him because we
haven't spoken since our misunderstanding about the
Christmas concert tryouts. Every day in science, I think
about saying something, but I'm too scared. He probably
hates me.

"You either have a really bad memory or a very for-
giving heart," I say.

"Why?"

"Because I don't deserve to get out of jail."

"Be c-c-careful," he says, "anything you say can and
will be used against you."

"Well, consider this a full confession. I didn't mean to
hurt your feelings last week. Honestly. I don't even *care* if
you stutter."

He smiles. He smiles big. I think I'm forgiven.

"Excuse me," Jorge says, "but I've got another warrant for your arrest, Lina."

"I just got out."

"I know, but . . ."

"Don't tell me, rules are rules."

He leads me back to the jail, but this time, I barely
step in when Luís bails me out. Five minutes later, Jorge
returns, this time with a warrant for Luís too.

"You must be really, really bad," Luís says.

"Who's doing this? I can't spend my whole night
in here."

As if to answer my question, Jason sticks his head through the jail bars. He's dressed as Rey Mysterio, a famous Mexican wrestler who wears a cape and a black mask with the profile of a golden eagle head. "Try getting out now!" he says as he walks away.

"You jerk!" I call after him. Then I turn to Luís. "Don't worry. Vanessa will get us out soon."

"It's okay," he says.

We sit quietly and wait. In the meantime, three ROTC guys get arrested. They're wearing their uniforms. They've got everything but the guns. The mariachi guy has been replaced by someone dressed as a royal guard for Buckingham Palace with the red coat, white pants, black boots, and tall furry hat. Like Jorge, he's in my history class where we saw a film about the guards last month. The ROTC guys try to bribe him for their freedom, but he's taking his code of silence seriously.

"You're talking to a statue," I tell them. "Give it up."

"We don't take orders from fish devils," they say.

"She's n-n-*nnnot* a fish devil," Luís says. "She's the *red tide.*"

I can't believe it! Finally, someone understands my costume. Last month, Mr. Star talked about the red tide, this algae stuff that travels along the Gulf Stream and kills lots of fish. That's why I have my poster with dead fish and S.I.P. tombstones.

"Whatever, piñata man," the ROTC guys say.

"Hey, he's not a piñata man," I tell them. "He's *kryptonite.*"

"Oh, yeah?" they say. "Whatever."

"You're the first one to guess my costume," I tell Luís.

"You, you're the first one to guess m-mine," he says.

"So I'm off the hook about the Christmas concert thing?"

"Hmm." He pretends to think about it. "Let's just say I'll be recommending you for, for parole."

Finally I see Vanessa walk by. "Hey," I call through the bars.

She turns around, and her eyes get wide when she realizes I'm still in jail. "You must *hate* me," she says. "I forgot all about you." She quickly pays the bail for both Luís and me.

"It's been almost an hour," I complain.

"I'm *soooo* sorry. I promise to make it up to you."

I'm about to ask where she's been when I see Carlos behind her. He's holding a big coffee can with a construction paper heart glued on.

"Hi, Lina," he says. "I'm the tin man. Get it?" He taps the tin can and shows me an empty quart of Quaker State oil.

"That's real cute," I say to Vanessa. "You're the scarecrow and he's the tin man from the *Wizard of Oz*." I can't believe she didn't tell me their plan about matching costumes. What else is she leaving me out of?

"It was all Carlos's idea," Vanessa says. "Doesn't he have a great imagination?"

"I'm sure your mom would think so."

"My mom?" She grabs my arm, takes me aside, and whispers, "Look, you can't tell my mom I've been hanging out with Carlos. You know how she feels about boyfriends. If she could, she'd send me to an all-girls school. She *hates* men."

I'm very tempted to tattletale after spending an hour in the jail booth. But Vanessa's my best friend, and best friends are supposed to cover for each other, even if one "forgot" to mention planning her costume with a boy. I look over her shoulder. Carlos is reaching into the neck of Luís's headless Superman. He pulls out a piece of bubble gum.

"Okay," I say. "I won't tell your mom about Carlos. You have to stay in the courtyard so they won't see you. Meet me here in forty-five minutes and we'll head back to the cafeteria together."

"You're great with the covert operations," Vanessa says, giving me a grateful hug before disappearing with Mr. Tin Man.

"Looks like I got ditched for Carlos," I explain to Luís.

He gives me this pretend frown. Then he points to the free-throw booth. For two dollars, he buys five free throws and wins me a glow-in-the-dark necklace. Then we eat turkey legs and *buñuelos,* my favorite cinnamon and sugar pastries. Then we try dunking Mr. Star in the dunking booth. Every time we see Jason, we hide, hoping he'll forget we exist. Luckily, he does.

Soon our forty-five minutes is over. When Vanessa and I return to the cafeteria, my dad and Ms. Cantu are taking down the Halloween decorations.

"We sold out!" Ms. Cantu announces.

I can tell because there's confetti all over the floor.

"I think we should celebrate," my dad says. "Let's go out to eat."

Vanessa and I start hopping like kids in a candy store.

"Can we go to Snoopy's?" we ask.

My dad winces. At first I wonder what's wrong with Snoopy's, then I remember how far it is.

"Of course," Ms. Cantu says. "I'll drive. How about it, Homero?"

He says "sure" — not with any excitement but like someone who doesn't want to spoil the party.

We get in Ms. Cantu's big truck. She's got the kind with an extended cab. Vanessa sits up front with her mom, while my dad and I squeeze into the back. As soon as we hit the road, he asks about *Watership Down*. He wants to know what the rabbits are up to.

"Have they met those complacent rabbits yet?"

"Yeah," I say, even though I don't know what "complacent" means.

That's enough to get him started on another lecture. Doesn't he know I'm taking other classes too? Doesn't he care? I'm grateful he helped with the carnival, and I'm *really* grateful we're going to Snoopy's, but this is my free time, time to talk about anything and everything *except school.* Mom would have known better. She'd have her fingernails painted orange and black, and instead of talking about homework, she'd ask about the games I played, the food I ate, and the costumes I saw.

I tune Dad out, and when he notices, he stops talking. All we hear is Ms. Cantu bragging about her *cascarones.*

"Maybe I should open a flea market booth," she says. "I can call it Cascarones Corner."

Then we get past Flour Bluff and reach the strip of road with nothing but the ocean on either side. I *love* living near the sea. I've seen pictures of mountains and forests and canyons. I can tell they're beautiful, but they don't carry the promise of a "forever" the way the sea does — especially at night when the black water and the black sky melt into each other, making me feel like I'm in the center of infinity. Tonight's a full moon, its light on the ocean like a glow-in-the-dark road. After seeing Vanessa and Carlos dressed as the scarecrow and the tin man, the light reminds me of that song from the *Wizard of Oz,* "Somewhere Over the Rainbow," a song about traveling across the rainbow to another land. That's how I feel about the moonlight. I want to walk on it and see where it takes me. Will it take me to my mother?

Finally we get to the bridge, and there below us is Snoopy's.

Snoopy's is a great place, right on the water. It has two parking lots, one for the cars and one for the boats. Inside there's a huge fireplace in the middle of the dining room. There's a dock along the back for people who want to sit outside. It's all very casual, no waiters, just an order and a pickup counter, a bar for the condiments, and lots of cats and seagulls begging for scraps.

Tonight they have a "Southern Special" on the menu, catfish and shrimp with a side of fried pickles. Vanessa and I order it, of course. We've never eaten the fried pickles before. They come sliced with a cornmeal batter, sour and crunchy at the same time.

Vanessa and I yap about the carnival. We're so hyped we talk with our mouths full. We're so hyped we don't notice how quiet our parents are until we run out of things to say. Now that I think of it, this is the first time my dad and Ms. Cantu have been forced to talk for more than ten minutes. No wonder they're so quiet.

"Are we boring you?" Vanessa asks them.

"No, *m'ija*," her mother says. "We're glad you're having fun. It's just like old times."

Then it hits me — "just like old times." Now I know why my dad winced when I mentioned this restaurant. Mom *loved* coming to Snoopy's. There was a time when we came to Snoopy's at least once a month, all of us, my family and Vanessa's family. We paired off with our conversations — me and Vanessa, our moms, our dads. But this is the first time we've come since Mr. Cantu left and since my mom died.

Thinking about it makes me really sad. I start to get a lump in my throat, the kind that comes before crying.

"I'm going to walk down the pier," I say, wanting a moment alone.

They all understand and let me go without following.

The pier isn't very long but it's private and dark. I get to the end of it and sit on the edge, my feet dangling over the water. Little waves splash against the posts. My tears plop into the ocean. I've tasted tears before. They're salty, just like the water below, and I wonder if the ocean is made of tears from all the people and all the animals that have lost their mothers.

After a while, my dad comes and sits beside me.

"I miss her," I say.

He says, "I miss her too, *m'ija.*"

Then he puts his arm around me and we spend a few minutes filling the ocean together.

Fragile as Eggshells

The day after Halloween is *El Día de los Muertos,* The Day of the Dead, a time when the spirits return, not to haunt us, but to visit. And, of course, that means Dad and I will spend some time with my mom. And since it's the first time we'll be honoring my mother, we want to make it extra special.

First my dad drives to La Guadalupana Bakery and buys skull-shaped sugar cookies. Then he stops at a flower shop and buys marigolds in a pot covered with blue aluminum foil and a dozen pink roses.

When we get to the cemetery, hundreds of people are already there. Most are picnicking by the tombstones. Some are raking away the leaves and watering the grass.

They say hello as we walk by. Then we reach Mom's stone, where Dad and I kneel to say a few prayers. When we're finished, Dad offers the roses to Mom's spirit, and I offer the marigolds. Then we sit on the grass and eat the skull cookies.

"Did I tell you?" Dad says to Mom. "Lina won her volleyball game last week. *M'ija* was the best player on the team."

"He's biased," I say. "Don't believe him."

"You'd be real proud of our daughter, *mi amor*. She's a smart one, too."

"Especially in science," I brag.

Dad has a few more things to say to Mom. I can tell he wants to be alone, so I go for a walk.

Some of the tombstones have pictures of the dead, but I don't need a picture to remember every detail about my mom. She loved jangling bracelets and sleeveless tops because she had beautiful arms. Most ladies have a lot of flab above the elbows. But not Mom. She had small cups of muscle on her shoulders and firm biceps because she exercised with her five-pound dumbbells every morning. She used to flex her muscles in the mirror when she thought she was alone. Sometimes I called her Xena from the TV show.

One thing Mom and Dad shared were *dichos,* but they were very different about *when* they gave me their words of wisdom.

Dad's, I admit, always made sense. They flowed from

the conversation. I might ask a nosy question, and Dad would say, "*No preguntes lo que no te importa*," which means "Mind your own business." Most of the time, his *dichos* were the result of something I did, usually something naughty. He might find out I lied, for example, and say, "*Las mentiras no tienen pies*," or, "Lies don't have feet so they can't travel on their own."

But the reasons behind my mom's *dichos* were always a mystery to me. She'd say them at the weirdest times, and they startled me because they were always unexpected, like the cuckoo of a clock that's ten minutes ahead.

One day, Mom and I sat on the back porch eating ice cream and she said, "*El camarón que se duerme se lo lleva la corriente*," which means, "The shrimp that goes to sleep gets carried away by the current."

"Mom, how did your mind go from chocolate ice cream to shrimp?"

She laughed. "That sure does sound like a gross combination," she agreed.

One day she was double-checking the expiration date on the milk carton and said, "You know, Lina, *lo mismo el chile que aguja, a todos pican igual*. Both the chile and the needle sting."

"Why did you say that?" I asked. "Are you thinking about mixing chiles with milk?"

"No. That would definitely give me a stomachache."

Another time we went to Payless inside the air-conditioned mall, with no way of knowing the weather, and for some bizarre reason, Mom said, "*Después de la lluvia sale el sol*." After the rain, the sun shines.

"Mom," I said. "We left the car in the parking garage, so even if it *does* rain, we won't get wet. I don't get it. Why are you always saying *dichos* when they don't matter?"

"They don't matter *now*," she explained. "But you never know when you'll need a good *dicho*. I want to make sure you have a whole bunch of them in your brain account."

"What's a brain account?"

"It's like a bank account, but instead of dollars, you save *dichos*."

I couldn't help laughing when I heard this, and even today, as I walk among the tombstones, Mom's silly way of teaching *dichos* still makes me smile. It feels good to think about her without feeling sad.

Every now and then, I glance in my dad's direction, waiting for him to signal that he's ready to leave. As I walk past the tombstones, I read the names and dates on them and invent histories for all the strangers, especially those who lived long, long lives. What would they be saying if I could hear them? Did they have daughters and do their daughters still visit?

Finally, my dad waves me over. He hasn't cried the entire day, but I can tell that his emotions are as fragile as eggshells because as soon as we get home, he rushes to his room and closes the door. The next morning, I find several wadded tissues in the trash, and I feel sad — not because of my mom, but because my dad didn't let me comfort him the way he comforted me at Snoopy's. When he hides this way, I feel like a burden and then I feel invisible. And I have to wonder, what's the right *dicho* for that?

Cascarones Factory

The following Monday, Vanessa peers down from the top bunk in my bedroom. "What's taking you so long?" she says. "We're going to be late for school."

I shrug as I search through my drawer. I know it's weird, but I'm thinking my love-life destiny is linked to socks.

"Is this about Luís?" Vanessa asks, reading my mind. Sometimes telepathy with your best friend is not cool. "Are you using your socks as love bait?"

"Maybe," I say.

"You're so corny!" She nearly rolls off the bed when she laughs.

"Quit teasing. It's not as corny as matching costumes."

"Okay, okay, we're even," she says, hopping off the bunk. "Move aside. I'll be your fashion consultant."

We decide on white knee-highs with pastel flowers embroidered up the leg. A very dainty design.

"I don't know why I try so hard," I say. "There's not much I can do about my looks."

"Quit acting silly. You look adorable."

"That's easy for you to say. You make zits look like accessories."

"What you need is a skirt," she suggests.

"No way. I'm too skinny."

"No you're not. You're just like my mom. Always hiding your figure."

"*What* figure? You've seen my legs. My kneecaps are wider than my thighs!"

She shakes her head as if I'm crazy.

By the time I get to science, my stomach is in a nervous knot. Luís and I had a great time at the carnival, but he hasn't exactly confessed true love. Does he like me or not? I wonder. When he comes in, he does his routine — sits in front of me, waves hello, looks at his sundial, and turns to the front.

Surely not the behavior of a boy in love.

Mr. Star starts class with a reminder about our semester projects, which are due right after the winter break. Then he pops in a National Geographic video about coral reefs and turns off the lights.

"Psst." It's Luís slipping me a note.

I try to read it, but it's too dark. I have to tilt it to the TV light. Little by little, I make out the words. *Can I walk with you after school?* it says.

Is this the sign of true love I've been waiting for? *Yes,* I write. *Meet me by the tennis court parking lot.* Then I hand Luís the note.

He reads it and whispers, "Okay."

The movie rolls on and just when I start paying attention, I remember that Ms. Cantu is picking me up after school. We're supposed to go to the grocery store, but I'd rather hang out with Luís. So I turn around to tell Vanessa, but she's in the back row with Carlos. They're not watching the movie. They're whispering to each other. After class, Carlos hangs around till the fourth-period bell rings, which means no privacy for Vanessa and me.

What do I do? I want to walk with Luís, but if I'm a no-show for Ms. Cantu, she'll call the Coast Guard.

With all this stress, I can't focus in English. To make matters worse, I haven't studied for the vocabulary test. Mrs. Huerta wants us to define words and use them in sentences. She calls the first task "recall" and the second, "application."

For once, I decide to take my dad's advice. He says I can figure out words by taking them apart, so I try it. The first word is *marsupial*. Okay, I tell myself, *mar* in Spanish means "sea," so a marsupial must be . . . seawater soup. FOR DINNER, THE FISHERMEN DIPPED THEIR POTS INTO THE OCEAN AND MADE MARSUPIAL. Number two, *trifle* has the prefix *tri,* which means "three," so trifle has to mean "full of threes." MY STUDENT IDENTIFICATION NUMBER IS TRIFLE. The next word is *felicity*. Now that's a hard one, but I notice that it begins with the same four letters as "feline." Hmmm . . . F-E-L-I must be the prefix for cats, so felicity must be . . . a city for cats. AFTER MAKING CARTOONS, GAR-FIELD WENT TO LIVE IN A FELICITY. Not bad, I think to myself. Before I know it, the test is done.

After school, I linger in the hallway hoping to catch Luís or Vanessa, but they aren't around. And no wonder! They're already at the parking lot by the tennis courts. Ms. Cantu is there too. What a major bust! If only I could turn back.

"Do you know this young man?" Ms. Cantu says. Before I can answer, she adds, "because he says you told him to meet you here, so he can walk you home." This third degree makes me feel like walking home's illegal.

Vanessa says, "Leave Lina alone, Mom. She can do what she wants. It's not like you're her parent."

"I kind of am. Did you know," she says to Luís, "that Lina is an orphan child? She lost her mother last year, *la pobrecita*."

"I, I know," Luís says.

"That makes her a delicate flower in my book. And delicate flowers have no business hanging out with weeds."

"Oh my *gosh*, Mom," Vanessa says. "Just because Dad . . ."

"Don't 'oh my gosh' me, young lady."

"Luís is not a weed," I say. "He asked if he could walk with me, and I said yes. I'll be home in fifteen minutes, Ms. Cantu. I promise."

"But I thought you wanted to go to the grocery store," she answers.

"I can go another time," I say.

We stand like cars in a traffic jam — each of us stuck and in our own little worlds.

"Well," Ms. Cantu finally says. "I wouldn't be responsible if I didn't get your father's permission first."

"Just let it go," Vanessa says. "She's not your responsibility."

"No she's not," Ms. Cantu says. "If she were, we'd be at the grocery store right now. Because no daughter of mine is hanging out with boys until she graduates from college."

Vanessa lets out this strange noise. It's loud and not loud at the same time — something part scream, part grunt. Then she stomps to the truck, slams shut the door, and sits in the seat with her arms crossed. She's angrier than I am. In fact, I'm not angry at all. I'm feeling a strange mix of embarrassment and appreciation.

"Hello," Ms. Cantu says into her cell phone. "Homero?" I hear my father's faint voice. "I'm just calling because Lina wants to walk home with some boy." My dad says something. "From school." He says something else. "Are you sure? Because I can take her home if you want. I'm already here." Another pause. "Well, if it's okay with you, but just so you know, this young man's Hispanic, five feet four inches, brown hair, brown eyes, and about a hundred and twenty-five pounds."

She says goodbye to my dad, snaps shut her phone, and says, "Remember, Lina, if you're not home in fifteen minutes, your dad's calling missing persons."

Finally, Ms. Cantu gets in her car and backs out. I wave goodbye to Vanessa, but instead of waving back, she turns away. Why is she so mad? What did I do?

When we're finally alone, I tell Luís that I live on Casa de Oro. He nods. Casa de Oro is only two streets away from our school.

"I'm sorry Vanessa's mom was so rude. I can't believe she gave my dad a police description of you."

"I don't think she's rude. She's, she's, she's funny."

"She *is* funny," I say.

He nods and makes the *loco* sign with his finger.

"She's a lunatic. I'm a delicate flower. And you're a weed."

He smiles. "A five-foot, f-f-four-inch-tall weed."

We giggle and then we outright laugh. The whole thing seems so ridiculous.

A few hours later, I go across the street. Ms. Cantu hardly looks up when I walk in. She's a one-woman factory cutting circles of tissue paper for dozens of *cascarones*.

"Is everything okay?" I say to Vanessa as I follow her

to the bedroom and take my seat on the beanbag. "You were acting a little weird this afternoon."

"Can you blame me? My mom's so strict. She'd *never* let a boy walk me home. She's such a man-hater."

"We need to change her opinion somehow."

"I know, but how?" Vanessa looks at the ceiling and touches her chin to brainstorm. "I got it!" she says. "Let's get on the net."

We move to her laptop, and I stand behind her while she googles "The Corpus Connection."

"What are you doing?" I ask.

"I saw this dating service advertised on TV."

"You're going to sign up your mom?"

"No," Vanessa says, "but I want to know who's out there. Maybe we can make up a secret admirer for her. That way, she'll be distracted, and she won't complain about my dad all the time. She might even stop making *cascarones* and let me hang out with guys."

The Corpus Connection Web page appears on the screen. SEE PROFILES, it says.

We scroll down the page.

"Look at all these dorky guys," Vanessa says. "This one sent a corny poem about his dog. 'My pet dog Peaches, sticks to me like leeches.'"

"That's gross," I say.

"And this guy's in training for the national cup-stacking competition."

"Is that when they get plastic cups and make pyramids real fast?"

"Yeah," Vanessa says. "And he's hyped. He thinks cup stacking is a serious sport. He thinks it should be in the Olympics."

"That *is* kind of weird."

"Hey, look," she says. "This one's looking for a señorita."

We read his ad: *Hello, señorita. I would-o like-o to meet-o you.*

"What a nerd," I say. "He thinks you can speak Spanish by adding an *o* to everything."

Vanessa closes the website. "I'm starting to think the Corpus Connection was a bad idea."

She pushes aside the laptop, plants her elbows on the desk, and drops her head into her arms. I wish I had the right words to cheer her up, but I don't.

Rotten Eggs

Another week goes by. After dinner every night, I go to my room. My dad thinks I'm reading *Watership Down*, but I do everything *except* read. As long as I listen in class, I can get away with *not* reading. Every day, Mrs. Huerta asks us to summarize a few chapters, and I always have something to say.

"*Watership Down*," I wrote on the first day, "is about a rabbit named Hazel." I got this detail from the book cover. "He's got two buck teeth and likes to say, 'What's up, Doc?' When he stands, he's as tall as a man, the tallest rabbit in his village. Sometimes the other rabbits make fun of him. He lives in a room underground, complete with a sofa, lamp, big-screen TV, Xbox, and everything a real house has except books.

Hazel's not into books. He's into carrots. He's always getting in trouble because he steals them from a bald man's vegetable patch. Last year, Hazel's mom died, and his dad ran away because he felt so sad. So now Hazel needs to find his father."

It's so easy to make stuff up when my dad gives me clues all the time. I'm not even worried about my grade. I figure I'm doing great because Mrs. Huerta still has my quizzes. She likes to make copies of the best assignments to share with the class.

Besides, I think the whole book's silly. Whoever heard of rabbits having intelligent conversations?

So, instead of reading the book, I rearrange my sock drawers, this time by theme instead of color. Then I take one of my lonely socks, slip it over my hand, and with a black marker, draw glasses and a nose on it.

"Hi, Luís," I say.

"Hello," my hand answers back.

I'm going to buy some yarn and add curly hair when I get the chance. For now, I put "Luís" next to my sock rocks.

I don't ignore *Watership Down* completely. In addition to my coaster, it's been my doorstop and weapon of mass destruction for every fly, moth, or ant that sneaks into my room. By now, the cover's got more squished bugs than the grille of my dad's car.

On a sheet of pink stationery, I write "Luís and Lina." Right when I draw a big heart around our names, I'm hit with a new revelation! Could it be more perfect? Luís and I have a fifty percent twin trait rate, which is my mathematical way of figuring out how much a couple has in common. Fifty percent is perfect because I don't want to be *exactly* like Luís. We need a few differences to spice things up. Then again, being too different makes for lots of fights while being too similar makes for too much boredom. So how did I calculate our twin trait rate? "Luís and Lina" — eight letters total divided by a twin factor of four (for the twin *l*'s and twin *i*'s in our names), which equals two — one hundred divided by two equals fifty percent.

On another sheet of stationery, I draw a T-chart, something my history teacher calls a graphic organizer. I write *same* on one side of the chart and *different* on the other. I'm about to make a list when Vanessa appears at the door.

"What are you doing?" she asks, hopping onto the top bunk and promptly checking her watch.

"Making a T-chart to list how Luís and I are alike and different."

She giggles. "Do you turn *everything* into homework?"

"Well, if this were a normal house, I'd be watching TV."

"Believe me, there's nothing normal about TV when your mom thinks Lifetime is a documentary channel."

"Is she watching another male-bashing show?"

Vanessa glances at her watch again, then nods. Just then, the phone rings.

"Aren't you going to get it?" Vanessa asks. "It's probably Luís."

She's right. Suddenly my heart starts racing.

"Well?" she says.

I pick up the receiver. "Hello."

It's a boy all right, but not Luís.

"Lina?"

"Yes."

"Is Vanessa there?"

"Who is this?" I ask. Then it dawns on me. Now I know why Vanessa kept checking her watch. This whole visit is a setup. "Is this Carlos?"

"Um. Yes."

Vanessa peeks over the edge of the bed and reaches for the phone.

I cover the receiver. "I can't believe you're using me for phone services," I say.

"Just hand it over."

She takes it from me and turns toward the wall. It's 7:45 p.m. At 7:55, I tell her to say goodbye.

"Just another minute, Lina. We're doing our homework."

Why is she lying? This is definitely a social call.

I try working on my T-chart, but I'm too mad. According to the best-friend code, it's okay if she uses my phone. I don't care. And I don't care if she lies to her mother, but I *do* care if she lies to me.

I write "Vanessa and Carlos" on a sheet of paper.

Thirteen letters with a twin factor of four. Thirteen divided by four is three point two five. One hundred divided by three point two-five equals a twin trait rate of thirty-one percent. They're doomed. It's in the numbers. They should hang up right now and save themselves the trouble.

I look at the clock again. Ten more minutes have passed.

I say, "We don't have call waiting, you know."

She peeks down at me again. "So? Are you expecting a call?"

"Maybe."

"Are you for real?"

"I'm *for real* about getting my phone back."

She rolls her eyes. "Hey, Carlos," she says. "I have to go now. Lina's turning this place into a whiner diner."

I can't believe she used "whiner diner" to describe me. That's what we say when there's a bunch of crybabies around. We use it when our classmates complain about homework or when our teammates complain about workouts, but we never use it for each other. Our motto is NO PAIN, NO GAIN.

"There," she says, handing me the phone. "Not that you're going to use it."

"You never know," I say. "Luís might call. He's been walking me home, remember?"

"Earth to Lina," she says. "He won't call because *he can't talk.*"

"He talks just fine."

"If you want to wait ten minutes for two words!" she says sarcastically.

Sometimes this friendship stinks like a rotten egg.

"Here're two words for you," I say. "Get out!"

Vanessa knows she's crossed the line with me because she apologizes right away and swears she didn't mean to pick on Luís, that it just came out. But I'm too hurt to forgive her. I grab *Watership Down* and decide to use it on the biggest bug in the room.

"Get out!" I say again, swatting her legs.

She hops off the bunk, runs out of the room, and I slam the door behind her.

Egg on My Face

The next morning, I walk out my door and straight to school. I admit it — I hold grudges. If only I weren't so lonely walking by myself.

Vanessa beats me to science. As soon as I enter, she says, "Lina, I'm sorry. I'm really, *really* sorry."

"Tell it to your boyfriend," I say, looking toward Carlos.

She lets out a little huff and leaves to sit by him.

I hardly look up from my desk when Luís walks in.

"What's wrong?" he asks.

"I got in a fight with Vanessa." I'm not about to tell him she made fun of his stutter, so I say, "About some girl stuff. You know how it is."

"I do?" He makes a big show of looking at his arms

and legs. "Because the last time I looked, I wasn't a g-g-girl."

That does it. He wipes the frown right off my face.

When class begins, Luís and I trade notes. He asks me things like what's my favorite music video, my favorite movie, the funniest thing I ever spotted on eBay.

"A wedding dress," I write.

"Why's that funny?"

"Because a guy modeled it, and he had a really hairy back."

Luís cracks up when he reads my note.

"Did I make a joke?" Mr. Star asks.

"N-n-no, sir," Luís says.

Before I know it, class is over and I'm feeling one hundred percent better. With Luís on my mind, I don't walk but *float* to fourth period.

Too bad I have to go to English. Mrs. Huerta squashes my good mood the minute she returns the vocabulary test — mine with a *big fat zero*!

"Please see me after class," she says.

"Okay," I say. "But while you're passing out papers, can you give me back the quizzes from that book we're reading?"

"No. I don't have them with me."

"You don't? Where are they?"

"Now, Lina, you know where they are."

But I don't know where they are. How can I concentrate with this mystery on my hands? Why should I bother summarizing the final section of *Watership Down* when

all my other quizzes are floating in the cosmos somewhere?

Maybe I haven't read the book, but like I said, I *do*
listen in class. I take notes too. I get enough details
for my Fiver and Hazel adventure. Fiver is, or was, Hazel's best friend. Last time, they had to wear disguises.
Hazel got mad when Fiver and a bunny named Carlita
paired up as the munchkin lollipop kids from *The Wizard of Oz*. They sucked on helium to get funny voices.
Then, they put on beanie hats with whizzing propellers
that chopped off their ears. For today's assignment, I decide that Hazel and Fiver are going to fight, a big fight
like the one Vanessa and I had. "The Final Blowout," I
call it.

After class, Mrs. Huerta waits for everyone to leave.
Vanessa hangs around, but Mrs. Huerta tells her to go
too. I'm still mad, but I have to admit, I wish I were walking out with Vanessa.

Once we're alone, Mrs. Huerta tells me to return the
vocabulary test tomorrow.

"With corrections?" I say.

"Now that you mention it, that's a great idea."

Why did I open my big mouth?

She goes on, "Return it with corrections *and* with
your father's signature. I think he'd be interested to see
how you're doing in my class and curious about why you
won't be playing any sports for a while."

"What do you mean?" I say, secretly hoping Mrs.
Huerta's using scare tactics. That's what teachers do

when they see a student slacking off. They throw out empty threats.

"I had to give Coach Luna a progress report for the new soccer season," Mrs. Huerta says. "You know the rules. House Bill 72 — No Pass, No Play. It's the law."

"I know. I'm really sorry I messed up, but . . ."

"No 'buts' and no 'sorries.' I don't accept excuses and I don't accept apologies. The only thing I accept is a change in behavior."

Her voice is dead serious. Oh, no! This isn't a scare tactic at all. I can't sweet-talk my way out of this. Today's the first day of practice, and already I'm getting kicked off the team! I get this big lump of fear at the base of my throat, and my ears and neck get hot with shame.

"But, Mrs. Huerta, I *have* to play. I have to keep in shape for the volleyball team next year." I'm trying not to cry, but a few tears leak out.

"No, sweetheart. You have to study. I know it's hard to accept, but you'll thank me in the long run."

"But I have to play," I say again. This time I don't care how kindergarten I sound. I start bawling. "Can't you give me extra credit? I'll do anything. I'll read a bunch of books. I'll wash your car. I'll babysit your kids for free."

"That's not extra credit," she says. "That's bribery."

Asking for sympathy from Mrs. Huerta is like asking for sympathy from an ironing board. She offers me the box of tissues, but I shake my head because in my purse is a "sockerchief," a white sock I use as a hankie.

I can't go to the cafeteria in tears. Everyone will ask what's wrong, and I'm not ready to tell the world I got kicked off the team. So I return to my desk. I try to calm myself using the positive self-talk my dad taught me. "You're okay, I'm okay," I tell myself, and "What doesn't kill you makes you stronger."

And what does Mrs. Huerta do while I'm sobbing? She eats a sandwich, munches on chips, and grades papers! She should be gassing cute puppies at the dog pound, not teaching.

I have to walk home by myself. Luís is rehearsing for the Christmas concert, and Vanessa's practicing soccer (not that I'd be with her if she weren't). I notice that all the kids who go home early are Hollywood extras, and then I realize . . . without soccer, I'm an extra too. I can't even be the water girl till I'm passing English again. The way I see it, I'm *lower* than a Hollywood extra.

I drop my backpack by the door and go to my room. It's been a bad twenty-four hours, the worst. I take a blanket, tie it around the posts of the top bunk, and let it hang off the edge, making a wall for the bottom bed. This is what I do when I want to disappear. I call my little hideaway "the cave."

Thirty minutes later, I hear my dad come in. He walks by my room and stops.

"Lina?" he calls. "Are you in there?"

"Yes," I say.

I hear him approach. He pushes aside the blanket and looks down at me.

"Why aren't you at soccer practice?" he asks.

"I'm not going to play after all. I don't really like soccer."

"Why not?"

"My legs are too long. I'll just trip over the ball. What's to like about that?"

I start to believe myself and why shouldn't I? It's true. All of it. Soccer and long legs don't mix.

"I wish you'd reconsider," Dad says. "Don't you think it's boring moping around while your friends are at practice?"

"No. I'm not bored."

"Hmmm," my dad says. I can tell he doesn't believe me, but he decides not to ask any more questions. After a few seconds, he lets the blanket fall and steps out.

Then I hear the phone. It's probably Carlos, but I don't budge. I want my dad to answer. Maybe he'll casually mention Vanessa's boyfriend to Ms. Cantu.

When I hear the mumbled tones of a conversation, I figure a salesperson called. Then, I close my eyes for a nap, but my dad calls me to the living room before I drift off.

"Apolonia!" I hear.

"What?" I call back.

"Get over here," he says. He sounds mad. He uses my full name only when I've done something wrong. So either I'm in trouble or a real pushy telemarketer bullied him into buying something like snow boots or a year's supply of mascara.

When I get to the living room, I catch him going through my backpack!

"Hey, that's private property," I say, but I'm too late. He's already found what he was looking for — my vocabulary test with the big fat zero.

He says, "Mrs. Huerta just called."

I can't believe it. It's like she read my mind, like she *knew* I was going to forge my dad's name. I am so busted. This must be what it means to get caught with egg on your face.

"She told me the real reason you're not at soccer practice."

What can I say? I just stand there waiting for my punishment like a sandcastle waiting for the tide to roll in.

He looks over the test. "How could you get a zero?" he asks. "Did you fail this on purpose? And why would you do such a thing?"

I can only shrug.

"'Felicity,'" he reads, "'a city for cats.'" He shakes his head. "How could you get 'felicity' wrong?"

"I did what *you* always do," I say in my defense.

"And that is?"

"I took apart the word to figure out its meaning."

"But, Lina, 'felicity' is like the Spanish word *feliz,* remember? *Feliz Navidad. Feliz Cumpleaños.* We use it all the time. It means 'happy.'"

"I tried Spanish with *marsupial*," I explain, "and I got that one wrong too. How am I supposed to know whether to think about Spanish or Greek or Latin or prefixes or suffixes or roots? And who cares about vocabulary anyway?"

My dad winces. He's really mad, but I don't feel guilty at all. Who cares if I let him down? We're even as far as I'm concerned.

"I just don't understand how you could be failing your favorite class," he says.

"English is *not* my favorite class. It's *your* favorite class."

He rubs his forehead. Good. I hope I'm giving him a headache.

"So what is your favorite class?" he asks.

"I talk about it *all the time*."

"Volleyball?"

"Volleyball isn't a class," I say. "It's an after-school activity. Besides, it's soccer season now, remember?"

"Math, then?"

"Math's okay, but it's not my favorite class."

I can't believe it. He's stumped.

"Science," I say. "I like science."

He nods. "I should have known. *Cada cabeza es un mundo*. Everyone has his own way of thinking. At least now I know why you dressed as a fish devil for Halloween."

"I was not a fish devil! I was the *red tide!* You never listen, do you?!"

I'm about to stomp to my room when the doorbell rings. Before we get to it, we hear Vanessa on the other side.

"Hurry, Mr. Flores! Hurry!"

"What is it?" my dad asks, opening the door.

"It's my mom," Vanessa says. "She fell down. She's really hurt!"

Egg Under the Bed

We chase Vanessa to her kitchen. As soon as I see Ms. Cantu, I think of the time I pretended my Barbie was Gail Devers, an Olympic track star. I had put her into the hurdling position and SNAP! her leg came off.

"Ay, Homero!" Ms. Cantu cries when she sees my dad. "I can't move!"

"Now, now," my dad says.

"I came home from practice and found her like this," Vanessa explains. "I think she's been here for *hours*!"

"It sure feels like hours," Ms. Cantu cries.

"Now, now," my dad says again.

"Someone gave me *el mal ojo,* the evil eye — someone who's jealous of my beautiful *cascarones*. Now I have to call *la curandera* and tell her to put the egg under my bed."

A *curandera* is a folk healer. She can get rid of a curse from the evil eye by breaking an egg into a bowl of water and leaving it under the bed while the victim sleeps.

"You don't need a *curandera*," Vanessa says. "You need a doctor. Please, Mr. Flores. Please talk some sense into my mom."

My dad reaches in his pocket for his keys. "I guess we have to go to the emergency room. That leg probably needs a cast."

Ms. Cantu almost faints. "*¡Ay, Dios mío!* A cast?"

When we get to the emergency room at Spohn Hospital, my dad helps Ms. Cantu to the check-in window.

"Why weren't you at soccer practice?" Vanessa asks. "Are you still trying to avoid me?"

"No."

"Then where were you?"

"Long story."

"I fell down in the kitchen," we hear Ms. Cantu say. "And I was *all alone* because my husband, that good-for-nothing, left me three years ago."

"Does she have to tell *everyone* she's divorced?" Vanessa says.

"Give her a break. She's in a lot of pain right now."

"I know, but I *hate* when she complains about my dad."

"At least she isn't mean to his face," I say.

"Are you talking about my mom or me?" she asks. "Are you still mad about me using your phone last night?"

"No, I'm mad about you making fun of Luís."

"So I said something sassy. I didn't mean it, and I told you I was sorry, didn't I? What else am I supposed to do?"

I don't have an answer, so I do the only thing I *can* do — sit in the chair and sulk.

Ms. Cantu says she can't do the paperwork because of the pain. So my dad takes the clipboard and fills it out for her. Then he turns it in, and while he's talking to the receptionist, I have a vivid memory of this same emergency room, this same arrangement of chairs, this same everything from the night we brought my mom. They didn't make her wait. They took her temperature, and in ten minutes, she was in the ICU. I can't believe I'm here again — at this hospital where she died — from that germ that looked like a bunch of grapes.

Suddenly, I realize that the peanut butter and jelly sandwich I ate after school is still in my stomach, jumping as if my stomach's one of those inflatable castles people rent for birthday parties.

"I've got to go to the bathroom," I say, leaving everyone in the waiting room.

I go straight to a stall and throw up. Then I cry, blowing my nose with the toilet paper. This is the second time I've cried today. The first time was my fault. I admit it. I deserve to be off the soccer team. But did I deserve to lose my mom? There are people meaner than me, people like

Jason who still has *his* mom. This is when I wish life were like math, when I wish I could put numbers into an equation and get answers.

When I leave the stall, Vanessa's waiting for me by the sink.

"Have you been here the whole time?" I ask.

"Most of it. I figured you were thinking about your mom."

"Sometimes our telepathy scares me."

"And sometimes the way we're mean scares me. What I said about Luís was terrible," she admits. "I'm just *sooo* sorry. I hate when we fight."

"I'm sorry too. I shouldn't have been rude when you tried to apologize this morning."

"No, *I'm* the one who's sorry."

"No, really, Vanessa, *I* am."

We smile a little.

"Is this a Lifetime show or what?" she says.

I nod. And then I laugh. We both laugh. Then we give each other a let's-make-up hug and go back to the waiting room, best friends again.

"Where's my mom?" Vanessa asks my dad.

He points to a hallway. "She took some X-rays. Now she's waiting in a room for the results. You can wait with her if you'd like."

"X-rays?" I say. "I *love* X-rays. I bet I could name all the leg bones after spending so much time with my *Gray's Anatomy* book — the tibia, the femur, the patella."

"Wait a minute," my dad says. "We're not finished,

young lady. We still need to talk about your English grade."

I look longingly after Vanessa, wishing I could join her and the X-rays. When I look at my dad, he's pointing for me to sit down, so I take a seat, wondering if I should fake a seizure because having a needle in my arm and a tube up my nose is better than getting scolded.

"I was thinking about what you said," he begins.

Oh, no. What did I say? When will I remember my mom's favorite advice? *El silencio es oro,* or silence is golden. If I accidentally said a cuss word, I'm in really, *really* bad trouble. I could be grounded for a year. Once I used a cuss word, and my dad said, "Get thee to a nunnery!" He was serious. I straightened up fast. Nuns are really sweet and I'm sure they're happy knowing they've got tickets to heaven, but they can't be athletes and they can't date boys.

"Maybe you're right," my dad says, pulling me back to the moment. "How can I expect you to show an interest in the things I like when I'm not showing an interest in the things *you* like?"

I nod, remembering how he read a book at my volleyball game, how he left the dinner table to search for *Watership Down.*

"So tell me," he says, "how can I help you with science? I'm sure I've got some interesting books in my library."

I'm flabbergasted. I can't believe my luck. I expected prison chains and a dungeon with roaches climbing the walls. Instead, my dad wants to help me with my project. That's great.

On second thought, maybe it isn't so great. How's he supposed to help? In some ways, my dad is really smart, but if we're talking about things that don't rhyme, he's lost.

"Any ideas?" he asks, still wanting info on my science class.

"I have to do a project," I offer. "On whooping cranes. The first birds have already started to arrive. Every autumn, they fly all the way from Canada to the Gulf Coast."

"That's a long trip," my dad says. "I think I've got a bird-watching book. Maybe we can make some posters."

"I was thinking we could see the birds in person at the Aransas Pass Wildlife Refuge. You won't see them around our beaches. They're very picky about their environment."

"You want to drive to the middle of nowhere and hike?"

I nod.

He thinks about it. I can tell he doesn't want to go, but after a few seconds, he says, "If that's what you really want. I can take you there the Friday after Thanksgiving."

"Really?"

"Sure."

"You can't act like a sailor from *Moby Dick* or like the god-of-the-sea guy."

"You mean Poseidon?"

"Yeah, Poseidon."

"What about Santiago from *The Old Man and the Sea*?" he teases. "Can I act like him?"

"No. No Santiago, whoever he is. And no *chupacabra* or donkey lady, either." Since we're going to look at whooping cranes, I add, "And no famous birds!"

I can tell this pains him, but he takes it like a man. "Okay," he says. "I promise. No sea or bird stories. No ghost stories either."

I can't help smiling. He smiles too and playfully tugs at my ear. Everything's going to be okay. I can't believe it.

A while later, Vanessa and Ms. Cantu, who's in a wheelchair, come out from the back room.

"How long will you need the wheelchair?" I ask.

The nurse answers for her, "Just till we get to the car."

"They're worried I'll trip over this big thing and sue them," Ms. Cantu explains, pointing to a cast on her leg.

When we get home, I ask Dad if I can go to Vanessa's for a little while. "She's going to help me correct my vocabulary test," I say.

He agrees. With Vanessa's help, I learn that a marsupial is an animal that keeps its baby in a pocket — a kangaroo, for example — and a trifle is something that is unimportant.

"Let's check the Corpus Connection," I say when we finish the corrections. "Maybe another dork posted his profile. At least we'll have something to laugh about."

We go to the laptop, and Vanessa gets on the net. Sure enough, there are lots of new profiles, but instead of finding a funny one, Vanessa finds one that grabs her attention.

"This guy calls himself the Silver Fox," she says.

We read. Under interests, he's written "traveling and cruising down Ocean Drive in my Hummer." Under job, he's written "businessman."

"He's got to have money if he's a businessman," I say.

"And if he can afford a Hummer."

"Click on his picture. The suspense is killing me."

Vanessa clicks on the picture icon, and the Silver Fox pops on the screen. He's got tanned skin, gray eyes, the whitest and straightest teeth, and silvering hair, of course.

"He looks like a soap opera star," I say.

"Yeah, the kind of soap star who plays the owner of a big company and buys his girlfriend flowers and takes her to Italy on his private jet." Vanessa stares at the Silver Fox for a moment. "This is it," she decides. "This is the guy who will make my mom forget she hates men."

"You can't actually contact him, Vanessa. That's dangerous."

"I'm not going to write to him. I'm going to steal his identity."

"What do you mean?"

"My mom needs a secret admirer in order to feel special again," she says. "The Silver Fox is the perfect secret admirer. So I'll pretend to be him when I write her love notes. What do you think?"

"I think she's going to hate men even more once she finds out he's a fake."

"But in the meantime, she'll feel better about herself," Vanessa says. "My mom wouldn't go out with some guy she doesn't know. But if she starts seeing herself as attractive, then maybe she'll be open to new relationships. See what I mean?"

"I guess," I say, still doubtful.

"She needs a positive experience with a man to fight off the bad experience she had with my dad."

"Well, when you put it that way, it makes sense."

"So you're going to help me, right?"

"Of course," I giggle.

An hour later, we copy the first love poem onto some pretty stationery:

I've looked up and down and in every direction
For a woman who's worthy of my affection.
But the girls I meet seem so fake,
Like people who want to make my heart break.
Then I discovered your love for art
And I know you're someone who'll take care of my heart.
So this Silver Fox gets down and begs
For you, the queen of lovely confetti eggs.

The Best-looking Egghead

Dad has always graded papers on the weekends, so Mom and I used to go to the mall or movies while he worked. Or we'd buy snow cones at Cole Park and watch the kids fly kites or skateboard. Now I just sit around the house on Saturdays, especially when Vanessa's with her dad. I get so bored. This is what I'm thinking when the phone rings. Lucky for me, it's Vanessa.

"Want to go to the beach?" she says.

"In November?"

"Sure, why not? We're not going to sunbathe. We're going to work on our science projects. My dad's lending me his digital camera. Isn't that great?"

"But there aren't any whooping cranes at the beach."

"Who cares? You can invite Luís and help him with his project while Carlos and I work on ours."

"Okay," I say. "Let me call you back. I've got to get permission from my dad."

Something tells me a Saturday at the beach is a no-no when I'm failing English. On the other hand, I've been working extra hard to bring up my grade. Every night, I read *Watership Down* and summarize the chapters. I don't know if Mrs. Huerta will accept these late quizzes, but it's worth a try.

"Dad?" I ask. He's in the living room, entering student scores on his laptop. "Can I go to the beach with Vanessa? Her dad's taking us."

"Sure," he says.

"And with Luís too?"

He looks up from his screen. He knows I've been walking home with Luís, and they've even met a few times. They get along, but that doesn't stop Dad from being overprotective. "You mean like a date?"

"If that's what you call going to the beach to work on projects."

He leans back in his chair. I can tell he wishes my mom were here so he wouldn't have to make such a big decision by himself.

Instead of answering, he says, "Under one condition."

"Sure. Whatever you want."

"Give this to Luís." He pulls out a business card from his wallet.

"What's this? A speech therapist?"

"She works with me at the high school. The students love her."

"But if I give this to Luís, he'll think I'm making fun of him."

"No he won't."

"Yes he will."

He takes a deep breath. "Lina, I can tell he's a really smart boy, so he deserves to speak well. There's nothing shameful about stuttering. It's a problem lots of people have, and it's something he can fix. So tell him to call my friend. She works wonders."

He gets back to his typing as if our conversation's done.

"So can I invite him if I promise to mention the speech therapist?"

"Sure, sure," he says. "As long as you're supervised." Then as an afterthought, he adds, "And take the extra key. I might be helping Irma when you get back."

I call Luís. I call Vanessa. An hour later, we're cruising in Mr. Cantu's SUV.

Maybe it never snows in Corpus, but the ocean wind sure gets cold. That's why I have on jeans, hiking boots, and a sweatshirt with a hood.

"That's a really cool scarf," Carlos says when he sees me.

Around my neck, I'm wearing the most colorful socks

from my lonely sock drawer. I've cut them open to make squares, then I've sewn the ends together to make a scarf. It's very warm.

"I can show you how to make one," I offer. "All you need are some old socks you don't use anymore."

"You might not like my old socks," Carlos says.

"Why not? Old socks have character. You can't just throw them away."

"Boy socks are a lot different from girl socks."

"How?"

"They're not as colorful," he says.

"We'll make you a white scarf then."

"I don't think I want my old socks around my neck."

"Why not?"

"Because they . . ." Carlos looks at his feet as if searching for the answer. "They kind of smell," he finally says.

We all laugh and Carlos's face gets as red as Mrs. Huerta's grading pen.

Everyone's dressed warm like me — except Mr. Cantu's girlfriend. Vanessa was right — she's a Windsor. Today she's got the spring-break look — a turquoise bathing suit with a floral sarong around her waist. She's got turquoise earrings, too. Her hair's in a bun with a flower neatly tucked in her ear — a real flower, something very Hawaii-looking.

She pulls down the sun visor to check her makeup. After a few minutes, she checks her makeup again.

"Do you really think your face has changed since the last time you looked?" Vanessa says.

"Behave," her dad warns, "or I'm canceling this trip right now."

Vanessa slumps in her seat and lets out a real bothered sigh.

The girlfriend doesn't say a word. Instead, she ejects Vanessa's CD. Now we're listening to some preacher guy on an AM station. What cold-blooded revenge. No wonder Vanessa hates her. She crosses her arms and stares at the back of the girlfriend's head with a look that could shatter bulletproof glass.

Looking for conversation, I turn to Carlos and Luís in the seat behind me, but they're using some kind of guy talk. All I hear is a bunch of "uh-huh's," "right, dude's," and some caveman sound I can't identify.

Finally we get to the beach. Mr. Cantu finds a nice spot and parks the car. There's a fierce November wind, but that doesn't stop the girlfriend from taking her umbrella out of the SUV. It opens, yanking her arm. Then her sarong flies off. She tries to catch it, and just like that, the umbrella takes flight, too.

"Walter! Walter!" she calls to Vanessa's dad.

He hurries after her things, and that's when I notice that he's wearing what looks like a golfing outfit — a yellow polo shirt with lime green slacks.

"I can't believe it," Vanessa says. "My dad is such a cliché!"

"What do you mean?" Carlos asks.

"He's almost forty and his girlfriend's only twenty-five."

"She can't be twenty-five," I say.

"She *is*. I went through her wallet to check her ID. She turned twenty-five *two months ago*! Leave it to my dad to have a midlife crisis. I'm surprised he isn't driving a convertible. I'm surprised he hasn't had liposuction yet. I'm surprised . . ."

I don't know what else she says. I'm laughing too hard. Carlos and Luís are laughing too. Vanessa stops midsentence, and then *she* starts laughing.

"It's so ridiculous," she says through her giggles. "What did your mom used to say when an old movie star married a younger woman?"

"*Para el gato viejo, ratón tierno.*" A tender mouse for an old cat.

"That's right. That's what I think about every time I see my dad and his girlfriend."

Poor Vanessa. Her dad has a young girlfriend and a whole new wardrobe, while Ms. Cantu's stuck with nothing but the TV, giant T-shirts, and *cascarones*.

"At least your mom has the Silver Fox to cheer her up," I say.

"Who's the Silver Fox?" the guys ask.

"He's my mom's secret admirer," Vanessa says. "She's been getting a lot of love notes from him."

We giggle, and when the guys aren't looking, we wink at each other, our promise to keep the whole letter-writing scheme a secret.

*   *   *

After Mr. Cantu and his girlfriend return with the umbrella and sarong, Vanessa and Carlos get the camera and head toward the dunes. Finally, I'm left alone with Luís.

Most people think Luís is a nerd, but in my eyes, he's the best-looking egghead in Corpus Christi. He's put a lot of thought into his field research. He predicted the wind, so instead of bringing paper, he brought two small dry-erase boards. On mine, he writes "plastic," "metal," and "glass." On his, he writes "paper," "oil clods," and "other."

"We're g-going to walk a mile down the beach and mark each type of trash we see," he explains.

"How will we know when we've walked a mile?"

"I have a p-p-pedometer." He shows it to me. "I've already set it to my stride and tested it on the track to be sure it's measuring correctly."

We start walking. It's not the romantic scene I've been dreaming about. We don't look or act like beach lovebirds on perfume commercials. No, we're all business. I'm ten feet into our journey when I realize how messy people are. Actually, they're *pigs*. We see the usual Coke cans and potato chip bags along with weird stuff like a broken ukulele and a hand puppet that looks like it used to be Big Bird. Who knew trash could be so interesting? Especially when I consider the trash cans and signs that say DON'T MESS WITH TEXAS. They're really obvious. So why dump stuff on the ground? And what about the wildlife? I'm sure the turtles and birds have cut themselves on glass or gotten tangled in fishing lines.

My mind is racing with all kinds of questions. So when Luís says we've walked a mile, I'm surprised.

"That was fast," I say.

He looks at his sundial. "It's been half an hour."

He puts the supplies into his backpack, and we head back. Halfway to the car, we spot a log.

"Do you want to r-r-*rrrest*?" he asks.

"Sure," I say.

We use the log as a bench and sit facing the water.

"My dad really likes you," I say. Then, because I promised, I hand Luís the business card. "He wants you to call her."

"A s-s-speech therapist?"

"Yeah."

He doesn't answer.

"I'm not saying you *should* call her," I explain.

"I know."

"I don't mind how you talk."

"I know."

"You do?"

"Sure."

He believes me, and why shouldn't he? It's true. I think about *Rudolf the Red-Nosed Reindeer,* the scene with the elf that wants to fix teeth instead of toys. Rudolf doesn't care, and the elf doesn't care about Rudolf's glow-in-the-dark nose. So if Luís is okay with my long, skinny legs, then I'm okay with the way he talks.

He draws a heart on the sand and writes our names in it. Then he reaches for my hand. I thought holding hands would be easy, but I'm not sure if my elbow should go in front of his or behind — or whether or not we should interlock fingers. We laugh because we look like we're playing patty-cake. When we finally figure out the whole handholding thing, we get quiet. We don't dare speak or look at each other.

Suddenly I forget about the beach trash and notice only the pelicans flying by. They look like dinosaur birds. I notice the waves too. I listen as they roll in. They seem stuck on a syllable, constantly repeating the "st" sound — *ssssT, ssssT, ssssT.* So, I realize, the ocean stutters too. I find myself enjoying the sound, the way I enjoy halftimes during soccer games because they make the moment last, because, while I'm waiting for the second half, I'm wondering how the game will end, and in this case, how the ocean's word will end — *ssssT, ssssT, ssssT* — storm, stream, stairway, stars.

When we reach the car, Vanessa's dad and his girlfriend are sitting in it. She's got the sarong wrapped around her shoulders. She's shivering, but that doesn't stop her from enjoying an ice-cold Coke.

"We've got snacks in the ice chest," Mr. Cantu says.

Luís and I dig in. After I go through a box of Cracker Jacks, a bag of Doritos, an orange, a few sardines, and a can of Big Red, Mr. Cantu asks me to get Vanessa from the dunes. So I head out by myself because Luís's lenses are too dirty from the ocean spray.

I spot the highest dune and climb it, my feet sinking

into the soft sand. At the top, I see how the line of dunes makes a fence between the coast and the flat grassland on the other side. I take in the whole scene, looking for Vanessa and Carlos. I don't see them, but I do see their footprints leading over another dune.

I follow the footprints, my feet sinking into the sand again. The higher I go, the noisier and cooler it gets. Finally I reach the top of the dune and there they are — Vanessa and Carlos.

They don't notice me. But then, I couldn't get their attention if I pulled their hair. That's how *involved* they are. They're holding hands the way Luís and I held hands, but they're sitting a lot closer. And then, Carlos leans over and kisses Vanessa's lips. Their kiss isn't long or intense, just a peck, but still — it's on the lips!

I don't want them to catch me staring, so I hide in the quiet bowl between the dunes.

I can't help it, but I'm jealous. If I gave into my mean streak, I'd stomp at the top of the dune and bury their romantic moment with a sand avalanche.

I tell myself I've got no reason to be jealous. But let's face it. I do! What about *my* special moment? What's holding hands compared to a kiss?

But that's not the real reason I'm jealous. The real reason's in our baby books. Vanessa grew the first tooth, said the first word, took the first steps. That's right! When it comes to growing up, she beats me to everything. In the past few years, she's had the first bra, the first period, and now the first kiss, while all I got was the first zit.

I decide to call out. "Vanessa! Carlos!"

A few seconds later, they peek over the dune.

"There you are," I say. "Your dad's ready to go."

After we drop off Luís, we head to Carlos's house.

"Are we still meeting at noon tomorrow?" Carlos asks Vanessa.

"If it's still okay with my dad."

"It's okay," Mr. Cantu says.

"What are you talking about?" I ask.

"Carlos and I are going to Target to buy some stuff for our project."

"Oh, great," I say. "I need to buy some film and a poster board."

"You mean you want to go?" she asks, glancing at Carlos. "Because it's not really a shopping trip. It's homework. You know, for our science class."

I can't believe I'm hearing this. Vanessa and I *always* go to Target together.

"Maybe we can go next weekend," Vanessa says.

"Sure," I say. "Next weekend."

I try to act like I don't care, but I do. When her dad drops me off, I say goodbye and pretend everything's okay even though I'm feeling like a sitcom that's been cancelled for a snazzier show.

Eat Quiche

Last Thanksgiving, my dad and I nuked turkey potpies in the microwave. We ate alone even though Vanessa and her mom had invited us over. We should have joined them, but it was our first Thanksgiving without Mom, and somehow my dad and I knew we couldn't let ourselves have fun. I still miss my mom's turkey stuffing with the celery and mushrooms. But if she saw me moping around, she'd be mad. She'd say life's too short for so much sadness. So this year we accepted Ms. Cantu's invitation to celebrate at her house.

"I guess she wants to show her appreciation for all my help," Dad says.

He's talking about the errands he's been running for

her. Ever since Ms. Cantu broke her leg, my dad's been driving back and forth from the high school, the grocery store, and the post office. He even delivered some of her Avon products. And now, every time he cooks eggs, he saves the shells, and when he has a dozen, he delivers them to Ms. Cantu.

We cross the street to Vanessa's house around three in the afternoon.

"Come in. Come in," Ms. Cantu says.

She's got crutches under her arms, but she still manages to greet me with a smothering hug — the kind where I'm stooped over while she pats my head and says *la pobrecita* over and over again. Today, her oversized T-shirt has a cornucopia with glittery fruit.

Ms. Cantu has set the table with candles, flowers, and her best china and silverware, which surprises me because even on special occasions, Ms. Cantu's a paper plate kind of person. She hates washing dishes and so does Vanessa.

"You two sit down," she says. "Make yourselves comfortable."

"Maybe we should help you," my dad suggests.

"No, no. We can manage."

When she leaves, my dad whispers to me, "Go and help them anyway."

I nod, happy for something to do. I go to the kitchen where Vanessa's taking a pie plate from the oven.

"I can't believe what we're eating," she says.

"What's wrong with the food?"

Ms. Cantu interrupts before Vanessa can explain.

"Okay, girls, take the bowls to the table," she says.

One by one, we take mashed potatoes, marshmallow yams, green bean casserole, cranberries, and biscuits to the dining room. Vanessa follows with the pie plate. Then Ms. Cantu comes in with some matches to light the candles.

"Well, that's everything," she says. "I hope you have big appetites."

"It looks . . . um . . . different than I expected," my dad says.

It *does* look different because there's a key item missing. "Where's the turkey?" I ask.

"Right there," Ms. Cantu says, pointing to the pie plate.

"That's turkey?"

"It's turkey quiche."

"That's what I was trying to tell you," Vanessa says. "Everyone else is having a *normal* Thanksgiving, but not us."

"Well," Ms. Cantu explains, "there's no way four people can eat a twenty-pound turkey by themselves. Plus, quiche is a great way to get eggs into the menu."

"But I'm sick of eggs, Mom!"

I have to take Vanessa's side on this one. I really like to eat weird stuff, but not on Thanksgiving. Couldn't Ms. Cantu make the quiche another day?

Once we're all seated, we hold hands to pray. "*Gracias, Señor . . .* ," Ms. Cantu begins. Then we eat.

My dad doesn't taste the quiche right away because he hates trying new things, especially new foods. But after a while, he takes a bite and then another, and then he gets a second serving.

"This is delicious," he says. And he's right. Everything's delicious, even the quiche, believe it or not.

While we sit around the table and pat our bellies, my dad says, "*Panza llena, corazón contento.* A full belly means a happy heart, *verdad*?"

"Very happy," we all say.

"I've got something else to make you smile." Ms. Cantu goes to her room and comes back with a DVD. "Here's a little Thanksgiving present," she says to Vanessa. "It's the first season of *Ugly Betty*. Want to watch it?"

"Do I want to watch it? What kind of crazy question is that?"

Vanessa hugs and kisses and dances around her mom.

"*Mucho cuidado*," Ms. Cantu says. "I've got a broken leg, remember?"

My eyes are as greedily big as Vanessa's. We *love* that show.

"You can watch it in your room if you'd like," Ms. Cantu says.

We go to Vanessa's room where I plop on the blue beanbag and wait for Vanessa to set up the DVD player. But she doesn't set it up right away.

"I've got to show you something," she says. She reaches

into a drawer and pulls out a Target bag. "Remember when I went to Target with Carlos last weekend?"

I nod. I've been wanting to ask about her "date," but she's been so busy with soccer after school. And in the mornings, my dad's been driving us since he has to chauffer Ms. Cantu around. So every time I'm with Vanessa, someone else is with us too. This is the first time we've had some privacy.

"After Carlos and I picked our supplies for the project," she explains, "we had some time to kill, so we walked around, and I saw this." She opens the bag and hands me a picture frame.

"It's the Silver Fox!" I say.

"No, it's some model dude. Don't you see the $2.99 in the corner?"

I look, and, sure enough, there's a big yellow $2.99.

"So that's why the picture seemed cut off," I say.

"The Silver Fox is a phony," Vanessa cries. "A big, fat phony! He's got to be *really* dorky to put a fake picture into the system."

I know she's upset, but I can't help laughing.

"What's so funny?" she says.

"You're mad at a guy who's a fake when the whole time, you've been a fake too. I mean, he doesn't even know your mom exists."

"I guess you're right," Vanessa says, sinking onto her beanbag. "At least things are getting better around here. My mom's been really sweet since she's been getting those letters. She wore regular clothes one day and cooked regular food. She even stopped complaining about my dad."

"So the secret admirer notes are working?"

"So far, so good," she says.

Vanessa puts the DVD in the player, so we can watch *Ugly Betty*. But something about a big Thanksgiving dinner and the sun going down puts us to sleep. We don't open our eyes till the ending credits roll.

It's dark outside, and when we get to the dining room, it's dark in there too with only the candles and the light from the kitchen doorway. There's an empty wine bottle on the table, a second bottle half-empty, and the strangest sound coming from the stereo.

"What are you listening to?" Vanessa asks.

"That's what I've been wondering all night," Dad says.

"It's a didgeridoo," Ms. Cantu explains.

"A *what*?" we want to know.

"A long bamboo trumpet made by Australian aborigines," Ms. Cantu says.

We don't even ask what "aborigines" are.

"I wanted to listen to piano music," Dad says.

"Everyone likes piano music, Homero. You've got to be more adventurous. Try new things once in a while."

"I guess you're right," Dad says to Ms. Cantu. Then he turns to me. "Come on, Lina. Time to go home."

"Don't forget your little gift." Ms. Cantu hands my dad something.

"What's that?" Vanessa asks.

"This?" My dad shows it to us. "Your mom gave me a CD with Native American music."

"They make wonderful sounds with animal bones."

"I can hear the coyote already," Dad says.

"Or a fox," Ms. Cantu adds. "A *silver* fox."

Did I hear correctly? Did Ms. Cantu say silver fox? Maybe I'm wrong, but my guts are screaming — she thinks my dad's been writing those poems!

I bite my lower lip. Every muscle in my body tightens up. No *cascarón* could survive my clenched fist. I can't believe what I'm seeing. Ms. Cantu winking at my dad and Vanessa with the biggest smile.

> Perro que no camina no encuentra hueso –
> *The dog that doesn't walk doesn't find the bone*

16

Kidnapped Eggs

The next morning, my dad, Vanessa, and I head to Aransas Pass Wildlife Refuge. It's a cloudy day, the air cool enough for sweaters but not coats. I hope it doesn't rain.

At the entrance to the refuge is a visitors' center and a gift shop. I buy a refrigerator magnet with a picture of a whooping crane and a bookmark with a bobcat.

Then we drive to the observation tower and walk to the top, where telescopes are mounted on poles.

"When whooping cranes are born," the park ranger says, "they're reddish-orange, but they grow up to be white, with a little black on their wingtips and tails, and with red 'caps' on their heads. They always have twins, but the parents ignore the weaker chick. So scientists started kidnapping the extra eggs and putting them in the nests of sandhill cranes, a bird that eats the same kind of food. Sandhill cranes take care of *all* their babies." He points to the water. "There they are. Right at the top of that bend."

I follow his pointing finger to two spots in the water. I can't see any details because they're too far. I try the telescope and move it around until . . . there! . . . whooping cranes. Two.

One of the birds is bent over the water, searching. Then its beak darts forward and comes back with a fish. The movement is fast — like the jump-back movement of a yo-yo. The bird lifts its head, points to the sky, and lets the fish slide down its throat. Then it flaps its wings in a happy way.

The second bird's standing close by. It's very still and alert like a guard dog.

"Well? What do you see?" Vanessa asks.

"One just caught a fish."

"Did you know whooping cranes mate for life?" the ranger says.

We didn't know, so we shake our heads.

"Ah," my dad says, "so they understand. Love alters not with his brief hours and weeks, but bears it out even to the edge of doom."

"That's really beautiful," Vanessa says. "I bet you know a lot of love poems."

She winks at me, but instead of winking back, I make the sign for "zip it."

I look through the telescope again. After a few moments, the birds walk a little. Jason's right. Their legs are long — very long. And skinny. But somehow they manage to walk without tripping over themselves. In fact, they look graceful.

Soon they disappear around the bend.

"They're gone," I say.

"You can still see them if you want," the ranger says. "We've got a trail down there. But you've got to be quiet. They'll fly off if they hear you."

He points to the trailhead. I look at my dad, and he nods.

Before we head out, I check the camera to make sure the batteries are working. Then I grab the notepad and three bottles of water for the hike.

The trees along the trail are short. They look like overgrown bushes. Between them, leaves and twigs grow in a tangle with stickers and spiderwebs. But we have no trouble hiking. As we follow the trail, the sky gets cloudier. Soon the sky's completely gray.

"Look," Vanessa says.

She points to a bench and a sign that says SCENIC VIEW. We're on a hill, not too steep, but dense with the small trees and bushes. Below is a strip of beach and water where the whooping cranes walk in a slow, relaxed way as if they don't have a care in the world. I take a few pictures, but I can tell the birds are too far away.

"What's wrong?" Vanessa asks when she sees my disappointment.

"I can't get a good picture. The birds are too far."

"That's easy to fix," my dad says.

He stands up and steps past the sign that says STAY ON TRAIL.

"What are you doing, Dad? Don't you see the sign?"

"Forget the sign. We're not tourists. We're scientists. Besides, in Texas, 'no trespassing' means 'watch out for hunters and bulls.' You see any hunters or bulls out here?"

Vanessa steps off the trail too. "Come on," she urges. "This is fun. This is crazy. Besides," she whispers, "your dad's a silver fox, remember? He knows how to get around in the wild."

"Quit calling him that," I say.

"I'm kidding, Lina. Can't you take a joke?"

She doesn't wait for me to answer. She and Dad are going to the beach with or without me. I don't have any choice. I've got to follow them. Who knows what Vanessa will say when I'm not around.

Somehow Vanessa and I pass my dad. We're quiet, remembering what the ranger said about startling the birds. If I had a bad view before, I have a worse one now because I can't see anything through the trees.

Finally, I see the shore and the birds about fifteen feet into the shallow water. I step onto the beach but stay close to the tree line. I aim the camera, centering the birds in the view screen. What a perfect shot. I can already hear Mr. Star's praise. No pictures from postcards for me. This is the real deal — worthy of *National Geographic*.

I'm about to click my award-winning picture when the birds fly off. I click the camera, but I'm too late.

"I'll never get my pictures now," I say.

"Sure you will," my dad says. "We'll just follow the birds."

He starts walking along the shore, and once again, Vanessa follows.

"Where are you guys going?" I ask.

"To find the birds," they say.

Before I know it, they've got a good head start.

"We should go back," I call to them.

"Nonsense," my dad says. *"Perro que no camina no encuentra hueso."*

I know he's right. The dog that doesn't walk doesn't find the bone, but I cross my arms anyway, refusing to budge.

"Besides," Dad says, "I should be more adventurous, remember?"

"What are you waiting for?" Vanessa adds. "It's your project. Not ours."

We walk and walk. Soon the shoreline gets very rocky and slippery. We step into the trees with plans to continue along the coastline, but soon we're deep in the forest.

"He doesn't know where we're going," I tell Vanessa.

"Sure he does," she says. "He's like a fox on the trail of a rabbit. A silver fox. Aren't you, Mr. Flores?"

"Sure, sure," my dad says.

I grab Vanessa's sleeve and hold her back a while, letting my dad walk out of earshot.

"You better stop it with the silver fox and poetry stuff," I say.

"Why should I? Don't you get it? The Silver Fox was all make-believe, but your dad, he's for real. My mom must have recognized the stationery. I think she was with us when we bought it. And besides, your dad has silver hair and he loves poetry. This is a match made in heaven, Lina."

"No it isn't," I say. "They can't get together!"

"Why not? My mom's already fallen for him. I can tell. And your dad's a great guy. Just think about it. If they get together, we'll be sisters."

"They're not going to get together!" I insist. "My dad still loves my mom, and once your mom figures that out, she's going to send all her man-hating energy in his direction."

"Hey, girls!" my dad calls back. "Let's stick together, okay?"

"Sure thing," Vanessa says, rushing forward.

I can't believe Vanessa wants to hook up our parents. It's the dumbest idea in the universe. And what about me? Don't my feelings matter? If I tell her to drop it, she should because that's what best friends do. They take each other's feelings into account.

I'm too mad to talk or even pay attention to where we're going. But after a while, I realize that our hike's going nowhere.

"Okay, Dad," I say, "where arc we?"

He stops and scratches his head. "We're taking the road less traveled," he says. "Just a little farther."

"A little farther to what?"

"To that field over there."

He points ahead, and I can see where the forest ends and a grassy meadow begins. We're on the lookout for whooping cranes, but when we get to the field, it's empty except for an old windmill.

"Okay. Where's the water?" I say. "Whooping cranes like the water."

My dad does a three-sixty, then shrugs.

"You brought me all the way to nowhere? Are you *insane*?"

"Give him a break," Vanessa says. "He's doing his best."

I let out a real big, bothered sigh.

"So I'm guessing we're lost," I say.

"Apparently," Dad answers.

"It's not the end of the world," Vanessa says.

"Quit taking his side, Vanessa. Right now, this is between my dad and me. I never interfere when you're upset with your mom. Do I?"

"Whatever," she says, walking away until she finds a rock to sit on.

"That's no way to talk to your best friend," Dad says.

"But Vanessa's always taking your side, even after you get us lost."

"I just wanted to help you," he says. "I thought we could get close to the birds."

"The only way to do that is to get back to the trail."

He reaches in his back pocket and unfolds a map of the park. We join Vanessa, and all of us study the map, but it's very vague. It doesn't show landscapes or windmills, only the shoreline, trails, and roads.

"We're way off course," I say. "See how the trail circles around? It doesn't come this far, so there's no way we're going to find it. I have no idea where we are."

"If only we could figure out where the water is," Vanessa says.

"Good point. From the water, we can head west. Eventually we'll find the road, and from there we can walk north to the observation tower."

"Great plan," Dad says. "So which way is west?"

I look up, but with the sun behind the clouds, I can't tell. The water's too far to see or hear. It could lie in any direction.

"We have to make a compass," I say, half-expecting my dad to jump into action. When he doesn't, I remember that when it comes to Boy Scout things, he's got as much know-how as a blob of Jell-O. "Do you have the magnet we bought at the visitors' center?"

He nods, reaches in his pocket, and hands it to me.

"Now take this paper clip," I say, plucking the clip from my notes. "Rub it against the magnet about sixty times. Make sure you rub it in the same direction every time, okay?"

My dad rubs the clip against the magnet, while I take the lens cap from the camera and pour some water into it. Thank goodness it hasn't been a hot day, or the water would be gone. Then I tear off a piece of notebook paper small enough to fit inside the lens cap.

"Here you go," my dad says, handing me the clip.

I gently place the clip onto the floating paper and tug an edge, watching it pivot till the paper clip aligns itself in a north/south direction.

"It worked!" I say.

"Let me see," Vanessa says.

"You're amazing," my dad adds.

"I'm not sure which is north and which south, but if we head perpendicular to the clip, we'll either hit the water or the road. Then it'll be easy to find our way to the car."

We start hiking again. After a while, my dad asks, "So where did you learn how to make a compass?"

"You're not the only one who reads. I do too, but I read about stuff that's *real*. Unlike *some* people. I don't fill my head with silly ideas like talking rabbits."

He lets a moment pass, then says, "Someday, Lina, you'll understand. Maybe poems and stories can't teach you how to make a compass, but they can teach you about a whole lot of other things. *La educación es la única cosa que nadie te podrá quitar.*"

That's his way of telling me that no one can take away my education.

After what feels like ages, we find the road. We

head north to our car. We're a lot farther away than I thought.

"Maybe someone will pick us up," Vanessa says.

But no one picks us up because no one's around. It's a gloomy day. Only fools like us would choose this weather for a nature walk. As if reading my mind, the sky begins a heavy rain.

"My notes!" I say, full of panic. I put them under my sweater, hoping to keep them dry, but I can feel the water seeping through. When we finally get to the car, I see that my notes are ruined. My socks are mucky with rain and mud, and when I take them off, they stretch out of shape.

"This whole trip's been a bust. How am I supposed to remember everything I heard and saw without my notes? How am I supposed to do a presentation without pictures? I wish Mom were here!"

"I'm sorry," Dad says, putting his hand on my shoulder.

I'm too mad to accept his apology, so I inch away from him, lean against the window, and close my eyes. No one talks, so it's a long ride home.

Stubborn as a Hard-boiled Egg

Once a month, we dress up for Spirit Day at school. For Color Day, we wear red. For Western Day, we wear cowboy hats and boots. For Retro Day, we wear outfits from our parents' closets. But my favorite Spirit Day, of course, is Wacky Sock Day. So I wear a pair of knee-highs with green, orange, and yellow stripes. I wear them with flip flops to show off the separate sleeves for my toes — like gloves but for feet.

Everyone thinks my socks are the coolest.

Today Mr. Star wants us to report on our projects. Everyone but me has gone on successful field trips. My visit to Aransas Pass doesn't count, since I came back empty-handed. As I listen to my classmates, I suddenly realize that I'm not only failing English but possibly science too. At this rate, I'll be off the team for the rest of the year!

"Carlos and I got some real good pictures," Vanessa tells the class. "Close-ups and everything."

Sure, I think to myself, they got close-ups. Close-ups of each other's lips.

"And how about you, Lina?" Mr. Star asks.

"Well," I say. "You see . . . I went to the Aransas Pass Wildlife Refuge with Vanessa and my dad."

"We had fun," Vanessa says.

"I bought a magnet," I tell the class. "Then I went to this observation tower and the ranger said whooping cranes mate for life . . . edge of doom and all that. The birds went around the bend, so we tried to follow them but we took the road less traveled and got lost. And I never got my picture because the birds flew off. Then there was this big, empty field, no water anywhere, so I had to make a compass on the spot. When we found the road, it started to rain, and all my project notes got ruined. So I guess I don't really have anything right now. But it isn't my fault. It's my dad's. All of it. The whole trip was a bust. Just ask Vanessa."

"Did the compass work?" Mr. Star asks.

When I nod, he smiles proudly.

Adults can be so confusing. I just told him I haven't got anything for my project, but instead of being concerned, he seems proud about a compass that has nothing to do with whooping cranes.

After science, Luís carries my books and walks me to fourth period.

He says, "I uh . . . I uh . . . I wanted to tell you something. My c-c-cousin is having a . . . a *quinceañera.* I have to stand in it with another g-g-girl."

I can't help being jealous even though I know that for most *quinceañeras,* the guest of honor chooses fourteen of her best friends and then guilt-trips her brothers and cousins into being escorts.

Luís says, "I know that I'll . . . that I'll . . . I know I'll have to dance with that girl, but it's just one time so you want to come to, to dance with me all the other times?"

"Really?" I say. "Okay." Even though I can't dance.

He smiles, then he shyly looks at his feet — not a good idea in the crowded hallway. Before I can warn him, he bumps into Jason.

"Hey!" Jason says.

"Excuse . . . I . . . I . . . I mean . . ."

"You mean what? Spit it out, dummy."

"Quit talking trash," I say. "Luís is ten times smarter than you."

"I wouldn't know. Porky Pig talks better than him."

"No he doesn't."

"Yes he does . . . P-P-Petunia Pig."

"Are animal insults the best you can do? Because you sound so preschool."

Jason and his friends laugh at me. I don't know why, but apparently Luís *does* because he walks off without a word.

"Hey, wait," I say. "Don't mind Jason. He's a jerk."

"I know."

"Then why'd you walk off?"

"Because I can speak for myself. Even when . . . when Jason's around."

"So that's why they're laughing? I can't believe how dumb I am. Can you ever forgive me?" I pout to show how sorry I am.

He smiles and says "sure," then he gives me a quick kiss on the cheek. Right there in the hallway! I'm hoping for a follow-up when the tardy bell rings.

"W-w-we better hurry," Luís says, rushing to his class.

I'm already late, so instead of running to Mrs. Huerta's class, I take the long route. I never noticed the watercolor paintings in the hall before, pretty flowers and seascapes. I know it's impossible, but I can smell the flowers and hear the oceans as if the paintings were alive. If my dad quoted a poem now, I'd probably understand it. The whole world makes sense, and it's a wonderful time to be alive.

In fact, I could live off my joy forever if it weren't for Mrs. Huerta.

"You're late," she says when I walk in.

I take my seat and she continues with the lecture. As soon as I realize she's talking about Charles Dickens, I tune out. The view outside the window is much more interesting than Mrs. Huerta's face. Besides, I don't care about make-believe. My dad's love for make-believe is what ruined my trip to the animal refuge. Give me newspaper articles, vacuum cleaner manuals, the ingredients on a cough syrup box, *anything* but stuff from someone's imagination, especially if that someone is dead.

Like Charles Dickens. When did he die? In the 1800s sometime? He didn't even live in Texas. I know, because I read the first few pages of *A Christmas Carol*. The place Dickens describes is full of snow. How can I relate? The only time it snows in Corpus is when someone throws Styrofoam peanuts on the ground. Plus, instead of saying "my bad" or "snap!" Dickens says dorky things like "Bah!" and "Humbug!" And instead of tamales, his characters eat dumplings for Christmas. What's a dumpling? No one I know in Texas eats them. As far as I'm concerned, a dumpling is something a cow leaves on the ground.

There's no way I'm going to waste my time reading that book. Besides, I've seen the Mickey Mouse version a dozen times. Ghost of Christmas Present, Ghost of Christmas Past, Ghost of Christmas Future . . . blah, blah, blah. I thought talking rabbits were silly, but ghosts? At least rabbits exist in the *real* world.

Mrs. Huerta catches me daydreaming. "So what do *you* think about Scrooge?" she asks.

"The Mickey Mouse guy?"

"Mickey Mouse? What are you talking about?"

"I can't believe you've never seen the movie," I say. "Mickey Mouse comes out on *A Christmas Carol*. So do Donald Duck and Goofy. You get the whole book in thirty minutes. We should watch it."

Everyone but Vanessa laughs.

"I don't appreciate facetious behavior," Mrs. Huerta says.

"Well, I can't be facetious if I don't know what it means."

"It means you're one step from detention, young lady."

"Bah! Humbug!" I snap back.

Thirty seconds later, she hands me the detention slip. "Next word," she warns, "gets you a trip to the principal's office."

I don't want to face Dr. Rodriguez, so I keep my mouth shut. Mrs. Huerta directs her question to someone else and goes on with the class.

When I look around the room, several students smile as if they're proud of me, but Vanessa looks away, embarrassed. That's when I realize I'm reaching my Hollywood status again — but instead of Star Student, I'm playing Class Clown. Today, my behavior goes hand in hand with my wacky socks.

Del dicho al hecho hay gran trecho –
*It's a long way from saying you're going to do
something to actually doing it*

A Soggy Egg Salad Sandwich

I don't want to tell my dad about detention, so I lie and say I stayed after school for study hall to work on my English grade. I thought I'd earn points with that, so I'm surprised when he tells me I can't go to the *quinceañera* with Luís.

"Why not?" I say. "I'm old enough. I'll be in the eighth grade next year."

"Not the way you're going. You're failing English, Lina. And you're lying. You didn't stay after school to study. You had detention. Mrs. Huerta called to tell me about your behavior today. I'm afraid I have to ground you now."

"But I'm already being grounded," I argue, "from soccer."

"Well, I'm grounding you from dances as well."

"I'm going to make up all my missing assignments. I promise, Dad."

"*Del dicho al hecho hay gran trecho*. It's a long way from saying you're going to do something to actually doing it. Besides," he adds, "we already have plans that weekend. I promised Irma we'd help with a wedding. We're going to decorate the hall. She can't do it by herself now that she's in crutches."

"I don't want to help with the wedding."

"I already said you'd go."

"But that's not fair," I argue. "All my friends will be having fun, while I'm stuck working."

"Remember that the next time you feel like lying."

I can't believe he's being so strict. I run to my room, slam my door, hang an extra thick blanket from the top bunk, and hide.

The next morning, I realize that if I ever want to go out with Luís or play soccer, I'll have to get serious about Mrs. Huerta's class. So I show up on time and promise myself not to give any attitude.

Fortunately, she ignores me. I guess she doesn't want any more bah-humbug incidents. After discussing the book for a while, she gives us an assignment. Everyone gets to work. Even me. I take out a sheet of paper and put my name on it, but just when I'm about to start writing, Mrs. Huerta says, "Lina, can you run an errand?"

"Yes, ma'am," I say.

I close my book and walk to her desk. She hands me an envelope and whispers, "Take this to the counselor's office. You might want to take your books too."

I nod, get my things, and head to Miss Kathryn, the counselor.

"Hi, Lina," she says when I knock on her door. "Come in. I was expecting you."

She points to a cushiony chair and I obediently sit though it seems silly when all I need to do is deliver an envelope.

Miss Kathryn's office is big but crowded. She's got a wall of file cabinets, a little refrigerator, a desk for her computer, another desk with the telephone and piles of papers, and two chairs by the window with a nightstand-style table between them.

"Make yourself comfortable," she says as she searches through a box stuffed with manila folders.

"Actually," I say, "I'm just here to deliver this envelope from Mrs. Huerta."

I offer it to her.

"Sweetie, that envelope's empty."

"Why would Mrs. Huerta send an empty envelope?"

"She doesn't want to embarrass you in front of your classmates. Some people are very sensitive about seeing the counselor."

"I didn't ask to see you. I think you're confusing me with someone else. Mrs. Huerta was very clear when she told me to give you this letter."

"You can open it if you don't believe me," Miss Kathryn says.

I've always wondered what's in these top-secret envelopes, so I rip it open only to discover that Miss Kathryn is right. It's empty.

Just then, the secretary comes in with two sack lunches from the cafeteria. Without saying a word, she places them on the table beside me, walks out, and gently closes the door.

"Here we are," Miss Kathryn says. "Your file." She waves a folder with an APOLONIA FLORES label. Then she opens her fridge and says, "We've got water, Gatorade, milk, and Coke. Which do you want?"

"What's going on?" I ask.

Instead of answering, she hands me a Coke can — only it's not a real Coke but some generic brand that says COLA FLAVOR.

"I thought we could talk over lunch," she explains. "I understand you've been going through a hard time lately." She points to the lunch bags. "Tuna or egg salad?"

Suddenly I'm imagining straitjackets and wires zapping my brain. "Are you seriously going to give me a shrink session?" I say. "Because I'm not crazy. I'm failing English, okay. That's all. Lots of people fail English without having to go on fake errands to the counselor."

Miss Kathryn calmly opens her soda and gets comfortable on her chair. She's got a clipboard on her lap and my folder beneath it. It's a thick folder. I wonder where all her notes came from. Has she been tapping my phone?

Interviewing my friends? Using satellite technology to track my movements?

If I had a hole puncher, I'd make confetti out of my school records.

Miss Kathryn points to the sack lunches again. I grab one without looking at the label. I unwrap the sandwich and take a bite. It's egg salad, very soggy, the bread dripping with mayonnaise. It tastes gross, so I put it back. Then I open the potato chips, but they're crushed. The only thing worth eating is an oatmeal cookie minus the raisins.

"I understand you were an excellent student last year," Miss Kathryn says. "But now you're not doing so well in English. How does that make you feel?"

"*How does that make me feel?* Is that the best you can do?"

She scribbles in her notepad, unfazed by my attitude.

"And your dad?" she asks. "How are things with him?"

"Can I go to the cafeteria now? I don't like egg salad sandwiches very much."

"Isn't he an English teacher at Ray High School?"

"Yes. So what?"

"And Mrs. Huerta is an English teacher too," she continues. "I'm wondering if there's a connection because you seem to be doing well in your other classes."

"I seem to be, but I'm not." What am I saying? I should stop myself, but I can't. "Like in science," I explain. "Just ask Mr. Star. Yesterday he asked us to report on our projects, and I was the only kid who didn't have any notes or pictures or anything. So this has nothing to do with English or my dad. Think about it. I'm in middle school. I'm going through my rebellious stage. Don't kids go through a rebellious stage? I'll get over it, Miss Kathryn. I'll get over it today. I promise. So can I go now?"

"I don't think it's that simple," she says. "I've been reading your rabbit story."

"What rabbit story?"

"The one about the mother who died and the father who's lost."

She opens the manila folder and takes out my *Watership Down* quizzes.

"I don't know why you think I'm writing a story," I explain. "Those are quizzes I took in English. We were reading this book and we had to summarize the chapters."

"These aren't summaries, sweetie."

"I know. It's just that . . . that . . . well, to be honest, I didn't read the book. So when Mrs. Huerta asked us to summarize, I made stuff up."

"That's what writers do," Miss Kathryn says. "They make stuff up, and oftentimes, they make stuff up when they're trying to deal with an issue or a problem that they're having."

"I'm not trying to deal with anything," I say. "I'm just acting rebellious like I said. I know it's wrong, so I promise, whatever Mrs. Huerta wants me to do, I'll do."

"Good. I'm going to hold you to that promise. But I

want you to make another promise too. I want you to finish this rabbit story."

"But . . ."

She doesn't let me finish. She hands me the quizzes and shows me the door, so I hurry to the cafeteria before the lunch period ends. I desperately need to talk to Vanessa, but when I see her, she's with Carlos. I don't want the whole world to know my problems, so I pretend like nothing's wrong. But something *is* wrong. Not only am I failing and off the team, but, apparently, I'm crazy too.

Ms. Humpty Dumpty

It's Saturday, and Vanessa calls around twelve.

"Want to go to the movies?" she asks.

"I can't," I say. "I'm being grounded because of my English grade, remember?"

"What a bummer," she says. "If I can get your dad to say yes, will you go?"

"Sure. Anything to get out of the house."

We hang up, and two minutes later, the doorbell rings. I run to the living room. My dad's in his favorite chair. Today his face is a book called *The Stranger*.

"Hi, Mr. Flores," Vanessa says when I open the door. "Why are you sitting here when it's such a nice day outside? You're just like my mom. She doesn't go anywhere because she thinks she's all broken like Humpty Dumpty. All she does is mope around."

"She's moping around?" my dad says, worried. "Is everything okay?"

"Everything's fine. She's just bored, you know. A whole Saturday with nothing to do. It's not like she can drive around with her broken leg."

"Do you think she'd like to go out?" my dad asks.

"Beats hanging around the house all day."

"Maybe your mom should rest," I say. "Isn't that the best way to heal?"

"You have a point," my dad tells me.

"No, Mr. Flores. All she does is rest. She'll get depressed if she doesn't get out."

"You think?" Dad asks.

"I don't only think. I *know*."

I can't believe how sneaky Vanessa is about setting up our parents after the zillion times I've told her it's a bad idea. Before I know it, we're piling into the car, and just when we've clicked on our seatbelts, Vanessa says, "Hey, Mom, do you think you guys could drop off Lina and me at the movies while you go for a drive?"

"If it's okay with Homero," Ms. Cantu says.

"Sure, it's okay," my dad answers.

Of course he says yes. If he grounded me now, he'd look like the bad guy.

"I'm not sure I *feel* like going to the movies," I say.

"You *have* to go," Vanessa says. "Unless it's okay with my mom if I go by myself."

"No daughter of mine is going to the movies by herself with all those crazies around. Anyway, I've never heard of a child who didn't want to go to the movies. What's wrong, Lina? Are you feeling sick?"

"No. It's just that . . . well . . . I'm being grounded, aren't I, Dad?"

"You're grounding her?" Ms. Cantu says. "But Lina's such an angel."

My dad shakes his head in a disappointed way. "*Hasta el diablo una vez fue ángel*. Even the devil was once an angel, Irma. And my little 'angel' is failing English."

"Failing English? Is that all? At least she's not sneaking around with boys."

"I'm in Mrs. Huerta's class too," Vanessa says. "She's boring. No wonder Lina's failing. I bet if you were our teacher, Mr. Flores, you'd make English interesting."

"You'd have to ask my students about that."

"Come on, Homero," Ms. Cantu says. "Let Lina go to the movies."

"Shouldn't we all stick together?" I say. "You don't want to hang out with a man, Ms. Cantu. They're nothing but trouble, remember?"

"*Some* men are trouble, but some are okay. Besides, you'll get bored at the karaoke bar."

"What karaoke bar?" Dad asks. "You don't expect me to sing in front of strangers, do you?"

"It's one o'clock in the afternoon. No one will be there. It'll be like singing in the shower."

"That sounds like fun," I say. "Why don't we all go to the karaoke bar?"

"Mr. Flores," Vanessa says. "Will you *please* let Lina go to the movies?"

"I'm already driving to the theater, aren't I?"

I can't believe how gullible my father is. Doesn't he know he's being tricked? But what can I do? The only way I can protect him from Ms. Cantu is by tattling on Vanessa, which is the number-one way to ruin a friendship.

Soon we're at Tinseltown, a giant theater with arcade games, fourteen screens, stadium seating, THX surround sound, and really cute boys at the ticket windows. There are a dozen movies listed on the marquee and posters lining the outside walls. We have to eliminate four movies because they're rated R and one because it's a silly cartoon. The last thing we want is to sit in a theater with a bunch of preschool kids.

"I vote for the comedy," I tell Vanessa.

"I vote for the romance."

"Want to flip a coin to decide?"

"No, let's ask Carlos when he gets here."

"You invited Carlos?"

Before answering, she spots him. "Hey, Carlos!" she calls, waving him over. When he reaches us, she says, "So Lina and I were trying to decide which movie to watch.

Lina wants to see a comedy and I want to see a romance. Which do you want to see?"

"Uh, the action flick," he says.

"Sorry. It's not on the menu. Comedy or romance?"

Of course, he picks her choice. The poor guy's in love. First Vanessa manipulated my dad, and now she's manipulating me — *and Carlos*!

"I *really* don't want to see that movie," I say, deciding that getting tricked into being a tagalong gives me the right to insist on my choice.

"Okay," Vanessa says. "You can go to your movie, Carlos and I can go to mine, and we'll meet in the lobby afterward."

"You want me to go to the movie by myself?"

"You won't *technically* be by yourself. Lots of other people will be there."

Is this the same girl who lives across the street? My "best" friend? I can't believe she'd send me away so she can be alone with Carlos. Where's the fun if you can't make sarcastic comments about the characters or share a popcorn or laugh and repeat the funny parts? The best thing about watching a movie is talking about it afterward. How can I talk to Vanessa about a movie she hasn't seen?

I grudgingly buy a ticket to the romance, and now I *really* feel like a tagalong. If you ask me, *Carlos* should be the Hollywood extra, not me. He doesn't know Vanessa as well as I do.

When Vanessa, Carlos, and I get to the auditorium,

Vanessa sits in the middle and raises the armrest so she can scoot close to Carlos. *I might as well be in another aisle — or another planet. That's how far away I feel.* We're early, so we get stuck with the elevator music and the advertisements. Between the ads are movie trivia questions. Vanessa and Carlos guess at the answers. Not once do they ask for my opinion. *I couldn't get their attention if I stood and sang the national anthem.*

"I'm going to get some popcorn," I say.

But instead of the concessions bar, I go to the restroom. *Maybe shredding paper towels will help me work out my anger. Too bad this restroom has electric air dryers instead. What I need is a stress buster, a squishy ball to squeeze.* I reach into my purse where I find an extra thick sock that lost its partner last week. I make a sock rock, then I squeeze it with all my might. *It works wonders.*

After I've calmed down, I buy my popcorn and return to the theater determined to enjoy myself, but every time Vanessa whispers to Carlos or giggles like a lovebird, my blood pressure rises. I squeeze and squeeze my stress buster sock, but I'm still mad. When I get to the bottom of my soda, I purposely make slurping sounds with the straw.

"Stop making those noises," Vanessa complains.

"What's that?" I turn toward her and "accidentally" spill popcorn onto her lap.

"Hey, watch what you're doing!" she says, picking the kernels and throwing them at me. *Normally, we'd call this a friendly food fight, but not today.*

When the movie ends, we go outside to wait for our rides. Carlos's older sister is already there. He jumps into the car and as it drives away, he turns to Vanessa and mouths the words "Call me."

When his car disappears, I say, "I can't believe you dragged me on your date."

"How else could I get to the movies? You know my mom can't drive, and even if she could, she'd never let me go to the movies by myself."

"So instead of telling me your plan, you *use* me?" I say. "And you use my dad too? It's not my fault your mom won't let you have boyfriends till after menopause."

"Calm down," she says. "It's no big deal."

"It *is* a big deal. You tricked me. And then you practically ignored me for three hours. Maybe I should tell your mom."

"No, don't," she says. "You're supposed to keep my secrets. You're my best friend, remember?"

"I remember, but obviously you don't. My life is all messed up, but you haven't even noticed. You're too busy with Carlos." Before I can say more, my dad drives up. The last thing I want is to discuss my issues in front of him, so I'll have to finish this conversation later.

When I get home, I remember my promise to Miss Kathryn. I still think it's a silly idea, but maybe she's onto something with this rabbit story. So I take out a sheet of paper and title it "The Next Hazel/Fiver Chapter."

"Fiver doesn't hear anything Hazel says," I write. "He's still waiting for his ears to grow back after getting them whacked off by the beanie cap propellers, but even if he *did* have ears, he wouldn't listen. He doesn't write notes to Hazel or send telepathic messages anymore. Hazel's not sure if he wants to keep traveling with Fiver. What's the point? Maybe the journey would be easier if he traveled alone."

Love Eggs

The holiday concert is scheduled for the Friday before winter break. Luís has been practicing double-time. He's asked me a zillion times if I'm going. My dad gives me permission since it's a school thing. I'm supposed to call when the show's over so he can pick me up.

I put on velvet green slacks and a black V-neck sweater. For the occasion, I wear Christmas socks with glittery poinsettias. They look cute with my black ballet-style shoes. When my dad sees me, he smiles. Then he runs to his bedroom. After a lot of scrambling, he comes back with something in his fist.

"I want you to have this," he says. He unfolds his hand and shows me Mom's favorite necklace, a gold chain with an emerald pendant. I can't speak. If I do, I'll cry. He kisses my forehead, and then puts the necklace around my neck. It's beautiful.

I feel a sudden gush of appreciation for my dad. Sometimes he can be strict, silly or embarrassing, but every now and then, he does the perfect thing like giving me this necklace.

At Baker, all our events are held in the school cafeteria, which always smells like food. For the holiday concert, the art class made hundreds of snowflakes, which hang down from the ceiling. All the teachers wear Santa caps, and Dr. Rodriguez, the whole outfit, even the belly and beard. The shop students show off their wooden toys, brightly painted. I *love* the train cars and doll furniture.

"Hey, Lina!"

Goldie waves to me. She's saved a seat, so I grab a program and join her.

"Where's Vanessa?" she asks.

"She's with her dad this weekend."

Goldie nods. Then she opens the program. "Look," she says, pointing to the choir section and the "Holy Night" song. I can't believe it. I have to read it twice.

"Luís is singing a solo?" I ask.

Goldie sees the worry on my face and says, "I'm sure he'll be great."

Something tells me a disaster's about to happen. My dad's always saying "*Donde hay gana, hay maña,*" which means "Where there is desire, there is ability," but I'm still doubtful. Letting Luís into the choir is one thing. He can always stand in the back and lip-synch the words. But giving him a solo? Hasn't his choir director noticed? Luís stutters! What can be meaner than forcing a shy, stuttering student to sing by himself in front of an audience? If people laugh at him, he'll be crushed, just crushed. But maybe he'll surprise us. Maybe he won't stutter. After all, this is the season for miracles.

I can't stop thinking about it. I'm so stressed I crumple the program.

Soon the lights dim, and the curtain opens. The orchestra's on the stage. The musicians are supposed to be playing "What Child Is This?" and "Dance of the Sugar Plum Fairy," but their music doesn't sound any different from the noise they make when they're tuning their violins. A wind chime could do a better job. I feel sorry for them.

The curtain closes and out walks the mariachi group. What a difference! They're great! They've got trumpets, guitars, violins, a *guitarrón,* and tight pants with silver buttons up the legs. They're not nervous at all. They're pros. They sing *"Las Mañanitas"* and *"Cielito Lindo"* and, since it's Christmas, *"Noche de Paz."*

When the mariachis finish, the curtain opens again. The band has set up its stands and instruments. Even though the trumpets and bassoons sound like they're burping, the band plays better than the orchestra. At least I can recognize "I'll Be Home For Christmas" and "Little Drummer Boy" without having to look at the program.

When the curtain closes this time, the elf squad comes

out. It's made of teachers dressed as Santa's helpers. A CD of "Grandma Got Run Over by a Reindeer" plays and the elf squad does a line dance that cracks us up.

Then the curtain opens again. A cool, silvery glow lights the stage. The choir stands on bleachers. The first thing I do is look for Luís. He's on the end in the boys' section. He looks so handsome in his tuxedo.

The piano plays a few notes, and the choir follows with something that sounds like ghosts and waves and birds all at once. There are layers and surprise melodies that come and go and come again. I get goose bumps. I almost forget to worry about Luís's solo.

Sure enough, the choir director nods to Luís. He steps down from the bleachers and stands alone in the center of the stage. Then he takes a deep breath and begins. Believe it or not, Luís has a beautiful voice. Some people sing from their throats and others from their guts. Luís is a gut singer, which means his voice comes from a deep place — deeper than sadness or love. And I'm not saying this because I'm his girlfriend. I'm saying this because it's true. Not once does he get stuck on a word. Every syllable is perfectly placed and as rich as the best fudge. He makes us forget we're in the school cafeteria.

When he finishes, the audience needs a moment to return to Earth. Then someone in the back claps, then a second person claps, then a third, and soon the whole audience is clapping and letting out *gritos*, whistles, and shouts of praise.

Everyone joins the choir onstage — the orchestra and

the band members, the mariachis and the elf squad. They sing a hearty *"Feliz Navidad."* The end.

When the concert ends, I don't call my father right away. If I do, he'll show up before I can talk to Luís. So I wait in the parking lot.

When Luís sees me, he comes over and says, "Just a sec."

He runs off, talks to a lady, and points in my direction. She nods, says a few words, then walks away, her hand on the elbow of a *viejita,* a little old lady, with a cane.

"My mom," he explains when he returns, "and A-Abuela."

I make sure his mom and grandma are looking away, then I kiss Luís's cheek.

"You were terrific," I say. "I wish I had a recording so I could listen to you sing over and over again."

He smiles. Then he takes my hand and starts walking me home. There are lots of cars on the streets around the school, but Casa de Oro is empty. Once we get to where it's quiet, Luís pulls me to the side of a garage, but a dog starts barking. We hear a man say, "Who's there?" Then we hear the banging of two metal trash lids. The man must think his dog is barking at possums. We run to the side of the next garage, but this time a security light turns on. I feel like a fugitive caught by a cop's flashlight. We run again. By the time we reach the third garage, we're laughing.

But we settle down. Here it's quiet, dark, and private. Luís leans against the wall, pulls me to him, and kisses me. Luís and I don't exactly meet the Hollywood standard. First, the boys in movies never have to look up to reach the girls. Second, movie couples always close their eyes. And third, they *never* say "ouch!" when their lips clash.

Still, Luís's kiss is nice, and it'll get nicer with practice, something I'm really looking forward to.

"I have to hurry back," he says. "My mom's picking me up after she drops off *Abuelita*."

"Okay," I say. Then I realize something. "You didn't stutter."

He smiles. "I'm doing better," he admits before hurrying off.

When I get to my house, it's dark. I ring the doorbell. No answer. Strange, I think, because the car's in the driveway. My dad must be at Ms. Cantu's.

I know it's nosy, but I decide to spy on them. Truth is, I'm worried. My dad's been spending too much time with Ms. Cantu, no thanks to Vanessa.

I sneak to the side of the house where the kitchen is. I tiptoe through the bushes, and when I get to the window, I very carefully peer inside. My dad and Ms. Cantu are sitting at the table making *cascarones*. There's a mess between them. Ms. Cantu is pouring confetti into eggshells and my dad's gluing tissue over the holes.

He looks . . . how do I say this? . . . he looks like he's having fun.

As Ms. Cantu hands my father an egg, I remember something I learned about *cascarones*. They came from China, but instead of confetti, the Chinese filled them with perfume and gave them to their lovers. So instead of a dozen roses, people gave their sweethearts a dozen eggs.

I sneak past the window, go to the kitchen door, and knock.

When my dad answers, I tell a bold-faced lie. "I called," I say. "But no one answered. So I had to walk home by myself. In the dark."

He winces, but he doesn't say anything.

"Girls get kidnapped," I explain. *"All the time!"*

"It's true," Ms. Cantu adds. "There was a movie about that on Lifetime last week. A true-life story. But don't believe the TV, Lina. For every bad guy, there are a hundred good ones."

"Why didn't you call over here?" Dad asks.

"Because I didn't know you'd be here."

Ms. Cantu says, "Well, you were at school and Vanessa with her father, so Homero and I decided to grab a bite from Water Street Oyster Bar."

"She made me eat calamari."

"What's that?" I ask.

"Squid. Can you believe I ate squid?"

My stomach gets a knot. Fast-food joints are for people eating because they *have* to, but restaurants — especially with wine lists and squid — are for people eating because they need an excuse to talk. The knot in my stomach grows when I notice that Ms. Cantu isn't wearing an oversized T-shirt tonight. Instead, she's got a fitted sweater and a skirt. My dad's a little dressed up too. They planned this, I realize. They went on a *real* date. Now I know why my dad let me go to the concert. He wanted me out of the house so he could be alone with Ms. Cantu.

"Look at your shirt," I tell him. "You got glue all over it."

"Do I?" He looks down at the glue stain.

"You're so *messy*," Ms. Cantu teases.

My dad laughs at himself. "I'm like a little kid."

Then they both giggle. Everything is suddenly cute.

"You *are* a little kid," I yell. "What kind of adult would let his daughter walk home in the dark when all these kidnappers are about? Don't you ever watch the news?"

Maybe I'm overreacting, but I can't help it. First, I'm losing Vanessa to Carlos. Now I feel as if I'm losing Dad to Ms. Cantu. So I stomp out. I sit on the hood of the car like I did after the volleyball slap. I know my dad will follow. I know he'll admit his mistake and apologize. And I know that I'll hold my grudge with a grip worthy of a pit bull.

Dancing on Eggshells

The next day, my dad insists I help with the wedding that Ms. Cantu's been hired to decorate. I don't want to go. This is the night I should be at the *quinceañera* with Luís. Working for Ms. Cantu is Vanessa's job, but she's been with her dad all weekend. Now I'm stuck with her chores.

The wedding reception is at Moravian Hall, a place that smells like cigarettes and beer. It's got a low ceiling with a disco ball. A disc jockey sets up speakers on a stage that's only one foot high. Ladies in hairnets walk in with pots of *menudo*, a Tex-Mex soup made from the stomach lining of a cow. When I see the single girl on top of the cake, I realize that these people are too poor or too cheap to pay a little extra for a topper that includes the groom.

My dad brings in the boxes, then starts filling little bowls with peanuts and mints. Meanwhile, I dress the tables with linen, then put a candle on a mirrored circle for the centerpiece. The cake and gift tables are special, so they get ruffled skirts too. Ms. Cantu shows me how to attach them with pins, each about an inch long and topped by pearl drops. While I dress the tables, she dusts the flower arrangements.

"I'm going to help your dad now," Ms. Cantu says. She tucks her crutches under her arms, hops in a clumsy way, and accidentally drops the pins.

"Ay, Lina," she says. "I'm so sorry. I've made a mess."

"It's okay," I say. "You go ahead. I'll pick them up."

I get on my hands and knees. What a hassle. The pins are all over the floor. I need to crawl halfway under the tablecloth to get them. I know my butt's in the air, but I don't worry about it . . . that is . . . until . . . I hear a familiar voice.

"Lina?"

As soon as I hear my name, I scramble under the table to hide, but I'm not fast enough. A hand lifts up the table skirt, and there he is — Luís! I'm wearing tattered jeans, a sweatshirt with bleach spots, tennis shoes with red dust from the track, and socks from my sock heaven drawer, which means they're faded and holey and stretched out. I know it's not the nicest outfit, but I didn't want to get my good clothes dirty. How embarrassing to be caught in this ugly outfit and crawling around like a baby.

He laughs. "What are you d-doing here?"

"Helping Vanessa's mom with the decorations. What are *you* doing here?"

"My cousin," he says.

Now the cake makes sense. This isn't a wedding but a *quinceañera*. Leave it to my dad to get the details wrong.

Luís holds out his hand and helps me up. My hair's a mess and my elbows and knees are full of dirt from the floor. Meanwhile, Luís is in a tuxedo again.

"D-do you think you can stay?" he asks.

"Looking like this?"

He nods.

"But it's embarrassing. Everyone's going to make fun of me."

"So? At least you'll b-be comfortable."

He's got a point. I don't have to look like Cinderella to go to the ball.

"I'll ask your dad myself," he says.

"But I'm being grounded," I try to explain as Luís marches toward my father.

I stay back, too nervous to hear their conversation. They talk on and on. I had no idea they had so much in common. Finally, my dad waves me over while Luís grabs his parents and his *abuela*.

"Isn't puppy love sweet?" they say, smiling at us and making me feel like a cute monkey at the zoo.

Maybe my dad's feeling guilty about forgetting me last night, or maybe he's getting over my bad English grade,

or maybe he doesn't want to be a bad sport — whatever
the reason, he decides to let me stay. He and Ms. Cantu
are going to grab dinner (hopefully at Dairy Queen this
time) and return in a few hours to pick up the decorations . . . and, of course, me.

Soon the dance hall is full of people. Lots of classmates
from Baker are here, including Jason, who's escorting one
of the *damas*, the fourteen girls that act like bridesmaids
and are supposed to represent each year of the birthday
girl's life.

I sit at the table with Luís's family while we eat dinner. I can't think of anything to say, and my chewing
seems extra loud, as if someone put a tiny microphone in
my cheek. How can I *not* feel self-conscious when Luís's
family keeps smiling at me — the kind of smiles that make
me wonder if my zipper's undone or if I've got food stuck
on my teeth? At first I was excited about staying at the
dance, but now, I'm nervous. I'd do anything for the silence to end, but when it *does* end, I find myself wishing life had a slow-motion button because Luís's family
talks fast.

"Do you like school?" they ask.

"Are you planning a *quinceañera,* too?"

"What do you want to be when you grow up?"

"Are you excited about the holidays? We always go
to Mexico. What does your family do?"

"Do you make tamales for Christmas?"

"Yeah, have you learned how to cook? You know what they say, the way to a man's heart is through his stomach."

"*¡Ya!*" Luís says, laughing. "This is supposed to be a d-date, not a job interview."

"Oooh, a date," his parents tease.

"Well, *m'ijo,* go ahead and enjoy your 'date,'" his mother says. "Just pretend like we're not here." She winks at her husband, and he winks back.

Thank goodness the lights dim. The DJ plays some *conjuntos,* and Luís's parents leave the table to dance. It's not as awkward sitting around with his *abuela.* She looks straight at me with warm, honest eyes that make me feel as if she's my *abuela,* too.

"You must be a very smart girl," she says, "to see how special *m'ijo* is." She pinches Luís's cheek, and he takes her hand to kiss it.

"Now you two go and dance," she says.

"I can't," Luís says.

"Neither can I," I add.

"You young people! You're not allowed to say 'can't' till you need a walker like me." She shoos us away, so we head to a corner of the floor to study the dancers.

"How are you going to dance for the presentation?" I ask.

Luís shrugs. He seems a little worried about it.

When the song ends, his parents spot us.

"Come on," they say. "You can't stand here all night."

"But . . . ," Luís tries.

"Nonsense," Mr. Mendoza says as if Luís has spoken a whole sentence. "We're going to teach you how to dance."

They take us to an empty part of the floor.

"Put this hand here and this hand here," they say, arranging our arms as if we were puppets. "Now listen to the beat."

We listen to a country-and-western song.

"Is it a slow-slow-quick-quick or an even one-two-three?" they ask.

I have no idea what they're talking about, but I listen, and sure enough, I hear it.

"It's a slow-slow-quick-quick," I say.

"That's right. Now look. This is how you do the Texas two-step."

They demonstrate while Luís and I follow. It doesn't take me long to realize that we're making *T*s with our steps. Of course, Luís's parents are much more graceful. Somehow their *T*s are round and sweeping, while mine and Luís's are stiff and square. But I'm having fun.

After the song ends, the DJ puts on some Spanish music.

"This is a *cumbia*," Mr. and Mrs. Mendoza say. They tell Luís and me to stand side by side. Then they talk us through the steps. "Right step long," they say. "Left step short. Then left step long, right step short."

We try it. It's a little like skipping.

"Move your hips. Be movie stars," his mom says.

We try, but it's hard moving the hips and stepping forward at the same time.

"Get fancy," his parents urge while his dad spins his mom.

We try the spin too, but I'm so tall I practically kneel to get beneath Luís's arm.

After the macarena, the bunny hop, and a few more songs, the lights turn on.

"Okay," the DJ says, "we need all the *damas* and escorts to line up because it's time for the presentation." He does a drumroll and ends with the clang of cymbals.

Everyone lines up — the parents, godparents, grandparents, important neighbors, and finally the *damas* and escorts. The DJ plays a jazzy saxophone piece called "Europa," and when he calls their names, the couples walk under the heart-shaped *arco* and down the center of the dance floor. When they get to the end of the floor, everyone claps and cheers, then the couples separate and line up to watch the next couple.

When Luís shows up beneath the *arco*, I have to laugh because he's with a girl who looks like she's still in elementary school. Most of the couples are oddly matched. They look clumsy and nervous — except for Jason and his date. I hate to admit it, but Jason's popular for a reason. He's everyone's idea of cute — everyone else's, that is. My idea of cute is dark skin, curly hair, and glasses like Luís's. The next time I wish on a star, I'm wishing that Jason gets zits or nose hairs.

By the time the last couple appears, all the boys are

lined up on one side of the floor and the girls on the other.

I've never asked for a *quinceañera* because I could never act as girly as Luís's cousin. She's got a fairy tale dress with ruffles, lace, sequins, petticoats, and a crown. She makes the queen of England look like a peasant.

"And now presenting," the DJ says with another drumroll, "the beautiful, the elegant, Miss Oralia Cruz!"

We give her a standing ovation. When Miss Oralia Cruz gets to the center of the floor, she and her partner dance. They have the floor to themselves for a while. Everyone sighs about how beautiful she is. Then, one by one, the couples along the sides dance too.

That's it. That's the presentation. The lights go off again, and the DJ puts on some disco music. We all go to the floor and jump around like barefoot kids on hot cement.

Now I know the meaning of "time flies when you're having fun." Before I know it, the DJ announces the last song.

"It was nice meeting you," Mrs. Mendoza says, giving me a hug. Then she tells Luís, "We're going to walk your grandma to the car. We'll wait for you outside."

She helps *Abuela* from the table, takes the old lady's elbow, and when they're almost out of sight, Luís grabs my hand and leads me to the dance floor. I don't know if the song's a one-two-three or a slow-slow-quick-quick. It doesn't matter. We just hold each other and sway. I rest my cheek on his shoulder. I don't care if I have to stoop. I'm too lost in the moment — until someone bumps into us.

All of the sudden, we're dancing on eggshells because it's Jason. He didn't bother us the whole night. Why now?

"Hey, Luís," Jason says, "where's your ladder?"

"My ladder?"

"Yeah, the one you climb to kiss your girlfriend." He and his girlfriend laugh.

"S-s-*ssss*," Luís tries.

"So how long did it take to think up that brilliant insult?" I tell Jason.

But he ignores me. "So what's it like dating a girl who acts like a cage fighter?"

"I-it's . . ."

I say, "More interesting than dating a guy who wears his brains in his underwear like you, Jason."

"Do you fight *all* your boyfriend's battles?" he says. Then, turning to Luís, he adds, "Is she your girlfriend or bodyguard?"

Suddenly I remember the conversation I had with Luís a few weeks ago. Once again, I didn't let him speak, and now our Texas two-step has turned into a giant Texas misstep.

"I, I guess she wants to be my b-b-bodyguard."

The song ends, and the lights turn on.

"Guess the p-p-party's over," Luís says, turning to walk away.

"Just a sec," I try.

"Forget it, Lina. Really. It's okay."

When he walks off, I'm too ashamed to follow. I can feel his anger even though he's tried to cover it up.

"Hey, Lina," Jason says. "A guy and a girl go to a dance. The girl messes up. The guy runs out the door at the rate of five yards a second. How long does it take for him to ditch his date?"

I can't say anything. My voice went out the door with Luís. All I can do is run to the restroom to hide.

I stay there till the noise stops. When I come out, the DJ's packing his equipment, the janitor is sweeping the floor, and my dad and Ms. Cantu are undressing the tables.

"There you are," they say.

I give them a weak smile.

"You okay?" my dad asks.

"Yes."

"Because it looks like you've been crying."

"I wasn't crying, Dad. All that cigarette smoke. It irritates my eyes."

"Okay," he says, though I can tell he doesn't believe me.

We load the truck, and I sit in the back, wanting to disappear.

When we get to Ms. Cantu's, my dad and I carry the *arco* to her garage.

"I can take the rest of the boxes," I say.

"All by yourself?" my dad asks.

I nod. I really want to be alone, and unloading the boxes will help me feel better.

As I put the decorations away, I try to figure out my actions at the dance. Why did I interrupt Luís? In a way, I *am* like a cage fighter. I can't stand when people get teased. Without thinking, I jump to their rescue. But if I'm *really* honest with myself (and this is hard to say), I'd have to also admit that I get impatient with Luís. Somewhere inside me I wish he could just get the words out. I feel horrible for thinking this because I know stuttering's not his fault, just like being tall is not my fault.

This is what I'm thinking when I quietly enter Ms. Cantu's kitchen. I don't mean to be sneaky, but because I'm so quiet, my dad and Ms. Cantu don't hear me. They're in the next room, and since they don't hear me, they think they're alone. And since they think they're alone, they're having a serious conversation.

I quickly hide behind the door. I know eavesdropping is wrong, but I can't help myself.

"Come on," Ms. Cantu says.

"Irma, I said no, and I'm not going to change my mind."

"Just try it for a month. If it's not working out, I'm sure someone else will happily take your place."

What is she talking about? Is she making moves on my dad? After all, she thinks he's the Silver Fox.

"I've done enough new things already," Dad says. "I've sold Avon and decorated dance halls. I've tried listening to weird music, eating squid, and singing karaoke. And now you want me to do *this*? I just can't handle that kind of commitment right now."

"It's not going to last forever," she says. "Besides, the kids will love it."

No, they won't, I think. At least, *I* won't. I don't care what Vanessa thinks. There's no way I'm letting my dad get involved with Ms. Cantu. Doesn't she get it? He hasn't forgotten my mom. I know it's been a year and a half, but it seems like ten years or twenty years should pass before he even thinks of another woman.

I'm about to "accidentally" bump into the table and interrupt them when I hear my dad say he's got to go. He sounds upset and impatient.

"Just give it a month," Ms. Cantu insists. "I already told our friends at school, and everyone agrees that it'll be good for you. You'll see."

"You told the people at school without consulting me?"

"It's no big deal," she says.

"It's a big deal to *me*."

"Don't be mad, Homero."

"I'm not mad. I just — I made a mistake. I've been letting myself get carried away."

"That's the whole point," Ms. Cantu says. "To get carried away. I wish I knew this a year ago."

The next thing I hear is the front door opening and Ms. Cantu hopping on her good leg.

"Where are you going, Homero? Stay awhile. Let's talk about it."

But my dad's gone.

After a moment, Ms. Cantu closes the door. She sighs deeply, and I can tell she's disappointed. The last thing I need is to be caught in the kitchen, so I sneak out the back door. When I get home, my dad's talking to himself and searching the shelves. He pulls out the biggest, fattest book in his library. Something that will take him a long, long time to read.

No Eggs to Paint

The next day, I punch in Luís's number, but I chicken out on the last digit. I try three more times before I get the courage to let his phone ring. No one answers, so I leave a message asking him to call me back.

I can't concentrate on anything because I can't stop thinking about the way the dance ended. Then I remember the hearts in my *Gray's Anatomy*. They don't look like the hearts on valentines. Instead, they look like potato-shaped plums with fat straws stuck into them. *Real* hearts have holes, not from Cupid's arrows, but from big, bloodsucking tubes. *Real* hearts are reddish purple — like bruises. No wonder it hurts to love.

Only Vanessa can help. After all, cheering up is what best friends are for. And I have to tell her what happened between our parents. I can't keep news like that a secret, especially from Vanessa, who's been playing Cupid all this time.

"What time are you coming back?" I ask when Vanessa answers her dad's phone.

"Not till the holidays are over."

"You're going to leave your mom by herself for two weeks?"

"She'll be fine. It's not like I didn't tell her. She understands. Really. Besides, I'm supposed to spend vacations with my dad."

"But, Vanessa, we *really* need to talk. A lot of stuff's happened."

"Like what?"

Usually I'd tell the whole story, but I don't want my dad to overhear me.

"I can't discuss it right now," I say. "We need to talk in person."

"Then let's get together. Carlos and I are going to the mall later. Want to come? I promise it won't be like the movies. I feel really bad about the way I acted. You can talk all you want. I promise."

"I was really hoping you and I could hang out by ourselves. I don't want Carlos to know about my personal life."

Vanessa gets quiet on the other end, and I imagine that she's looking at the ceiling to come up with a plan. I know she doesn't want to miss out on time with Carlos, since her dad's okay with the boyfriend idea, but what about me? Don't we *always* hang out during the holidays?

"Well, there's no school, so we've got two whole weeks," she finally says. "I'll ask my dad to drop me off, and we'll spend a whole day together."

I believe her, so I wait for her to call and tell me when she's coming. But days go by before the phone rings, and when it *does* ring, it's a salesperson. I start calling Vanessa, but she's never around, and when she *is* around, she's already talking to Carlos on the other line. I stop being confused about Luís and start being confused about Vanessa. To make matters worse, my dad's been glued to this *War and Peace* book all week. I don't think he's reading, just hiding behind the pages. It's the most boring holiday ever.

"Let's drive around and look at the Christmas lights," I tell my dad. "Like we used to with Mom."

"If you want," he says.

I stare at him for a long time. He stays hidden behind his book. I don't think he really heard me. I could ask if he'd like to smash the headlights on the car, and he'd probably nod.

I wish Mom were here. She liked to decorate the entire house, even the bathroom — where she replaced the knickknacks and candles with her collection of snowmen figurines. I find the snowmen and put them up, but my arrangement doesn't look as nice. Mom's baking would make the whole house smell like cinnamon, apples, and vanilla, but I have to settle for scented candles now. Mom liked to cross-stitch ornaments. She didn't have a chance to teach me. But I take one out of the storage box and count the stitches because I know *she* had to count them, and somehow this makes me feel connected to her.

I feel so lonely for Mom. I can tell Dad's lonely for her too. But I'm here, aren't I? Since we both miss her, we should be helping each other out. And with me around, how can he be as lonely as he acts?

Now I understand why Ms. Cantu makes so many *cascarones*. It's therapy, something to numb the mind when it's too painful to think.

Since I have no one to talk to and no eggs to paint, I write. "Hazel's been walking alone. Finally he sees the sign to his father's rabbit hole. DAD'S RABBIT HOLE, it says. Hazel thumps his foot. That's how rabbits knock. He peeks inside. It's dark, but he goes in anyway, calling for his dad. The ground is muddy. Hazel's feet get wet. Every now and then, he feels a creepy-crawly on his back. Off the main tunnel are little side holes, like rooms. But each is empty. Soon Hazel hits a dead end. He turns around but hits a dead end again. That's when he realizes he's lost. He's so lonely. He calls out for his dad. He calls out for Fiver. But no one answers him."

Don't Count Your Chickens
Before They Hatch

Vanessa comes back the night before we return to school. As soon as she touches base with her mom, she comes by for a visit. I've been bottling things up for two weeks, so I thought I'd talk faster than a telemarketer when I saw her. But Vanessa doesn't give me a chance.

"Do you like it?" she asks, reaching in her purse and pulling out a silver ring with a little dangling heart.

"A lot of stuff happened," I try to say.

"Carlos bought it for me. What did Luís give you?"

"Nothing. We had a . . ."

"I shouldn't have picked on my dad's girlfriend so

much. She's nice once you get to know her. Guess what we did one day?"

"I will, but first . . ."

"She took me to a spa. It was so cool, Lina. Look at my feet." Vanessa takes off her socks and shows me pink toenails. "I got a pedicure. And then we . . ."

"I can't believe you spent a whole day with your dad's girlfriend."

"Why not? Like I said, she's okay for a Windsor."

"But what about *me*, Vanessa? We were supposed to get together. I kept waiting and waiting. Don't you want to know . . ."

"Are you jealous of my dad's girlfriend?" she teases.

"Yes. I mean, no. I mean, can't I say two words without getting interrupted? Especially since I've been wanting to talk to you for two weeks!"

"But we *have* talked," she says.

"Not really," I say. "Most of the time you talked about yourself or hurried through the conversation because you were going to the mall with Carlos or getting pedicures with your dad's girlfriend!" I don't mean to get so upset, but I do.

Vanessa spends a moment twisting her new ring round and round her finger.

"I'm a terrible friend," she says.

"The worst."

She puts a comforting arm around me, and we give each other one of our let's-be-friends-again hugs. It's hard to hold a grudge when someone's hugging you.

After a minute, she says, "I promise to keep my mouth shut and pay attention. So what did Luís get you for Christmas?"

"Nothing," I say. "That's why I've been trying to call you. Luís and I broke up."

"I know you had a fight. But you broke up? For real?"

"I tried to apologize, but he never answered his phone. I left a few messages, but not once did he call back. So I guess it's over."

"Luís ignored you for two whole weeks?"

I nod.

"Wait till I get my hands on him."

When she socks her fist, I can't help giggling even though I'm still upset.

"What's so funny?" she asks.

"If you get mad at Luís, you'll have to get mad at yourself because you ignored me too."

"I *am* mad at myself," she says. "I'm going to take away my computer privileges for two weeks. As soon as I get home, I'm going to fold up my laptop and hide it in the darkest corner of my closet."

"I think you better bring it over here," I say. "I don't want you sneaking in computer time when I'm not around."

She holds up her left hand and puts her right one over her heart. "Will do."

"There's more," I tell her. "Luís and I aren't the only people who fought. Our parents had a big blowout too. My dad's been ignoring your mom ever since."

"What happened?"

"It's like I said, Vanessa. He's not ready for a relationship. We shouldn't have let your mom think he's the Silver Fox. Now they aren't even friends."

"How could they stop being friends? They were perfect for each other." She lowers and shakes her head. "This is all my fault," she admits. "I've got to find a way to fix this."

With that she puts her hand on her chin, looks at the ceiling, but thirty minutes go by without a solution. And since it's a school night, she has to go home.

I told Vanessa I'd have to go to school extra early in order to see Mrs. Huerta. I might not be able to do much about my private life, but I can certainly fix my grades.

I put a mountain of makeup work on Mrs. Huerta's desk. She accepts it with a smile. "I'm glad to see you're finally taking an interest," she says. "Unfortunately, it's too late for soccer, and it might be too late for basketball, but hopefully you'll be passing in time for the track season."

This is the last thing I need to hear. I get that terrible lump in my throat, so I swallow hard, hoping to wash down my sadness. But it doesn't work. I'm like a vase that fell off a table and got glued back together. Even after Super Glue, a broken vase can't hold water without leaking from a dozen cracks. That's me. I might be able to swallow down my tears, but I can't stop my hands from sweating and my voice from getting choked up.

"I thought my makeup work would get me into sports again," I manage to say.

"Sometimes 'too late' really does mean too late," Mrs. Huerta explains when she hears my disappointment. "It's a hard lesson to learn, Lina, but for every choice you make, there's a consequence. And sometimes, there's no way to make up for lost time."

I nod, trying to be a good sport, but, inside, my heart is breaking. I really thought finishing the missing assignments would get me in sports again. I guess this is why adults always tell us not to count our chickens before they hatch.

After I leave Mrs. Huerta, I run to the counselor's office to give Miss Kathryn the Hazel paragraphs I wrote over the holidays. But even this doesn't seem to be enough. Miss Kathryn scans them, then tells me I have to finish the story.

"But I can't think of anything else for Hazel to do."

"You'll figure it out," she says, returning the papers.

So far, my morning's been a total bust, and that's because I haven't seen Luís yet. How can I face him? He obviously doesn't want to talk to me since he never returned my calls. I decide to wait till the last minute before entering my science class. The bell rings as soon as I enter, and lucky for me, Mr. Star gets started right away. Luís is already in his desk, and when he sees me, he smiles and waves. This is very strange behavior from an ex-boyfriend. I don't know what to do, so I kind of smile and wave back.

Today's the due date for our marine biology projects. Vanessa and Carlos decide to present theirs together since they're both dealing with dunes. I can't believe they actually had time to take pictures and gather samples with all that smooching they did at the beach. Their presentation actually surprises me. I learn that plants make dunes. According to Vanessa, thick grasses act like nets that catch the sand. When the sand covers them up, the grasses have to grow taller to reach the sunlight, but all they do is collect *more* sand. This goes on and on until the big giant dunes are formed.

For my presentation, I use the PowerPoint program. I tell the class how endangered the whooping cranes are and how there were only twenty-six one time. That really gets their attention. Then I tell them how the birds fly all the way from Canada to Texas every year. Not to mention their wingspan, which is over seven feet long. Seven feet! Compared to ducks or pigeons, whooping cranes must have been easy targets for the hunters. No wonder so many were shot down.

I know it's weird, but realizing this makes me feel better. If birds could talk, I'm sure the whooping cranes and I could have a good heart-to-heart about being targeted because we're tall. I once read a book about Indians that have animal spirit guides and decide that whooping cranes are going to be *my* special animals. So next time Jason sees me and says "whoop, whoop," I'm going to take it as a compliment.

When I finish my presentation, it's Luís's turn. He sets

up an easel and grabs several posters from behind Mr.
Star's desk. He's made bar graphs. Instead of coloring the
bars, he's made them three-dimensional by gluing on bottle caps to represent the glass bottles we found, scrunched
grocery bags to represent the plastic, and soda can tabs
for the aluminum and metal. First he tells us what kind of
trash is at the beach and all the bad things it does to wildlife. Then he tells us what we can do about it. Before I
know it, he's passing around a sign-up sheet so people
can volunteer to clean our shores.

At the very end of his presentation, he says, "I'd like
to thank Vanessa and her dad for taking me to the beach
and Lina for helping me measure the trash."

Why would he thank me when he hates me so much?
His behavior confuses me, so I don't hear the other pre-
sentations, especially when I notice that Luís is scribbling
away. Taking notes! As if nothing's wrong! I don't know
how I'm supposed to feel. I've never had an ex-boyfriend
before.

After class, I quickly grab my books.

"Wait up," Luís says.

"I can't," I say, backing toward the door.

I hurry out, but not before I hear Luís ask Vanessa
why I'm running away.

"Didn't you guys have a fight?" she says.

I can't concentrate for the rest of the day. It's impossible to tell what people are thinking, and when I *do* know
what they're thinking, they don't know what *I'm* thinking. So all kinds of stuff get lost in the space between my

words and their words. Now I know why my dad's always hiding his face in a book. There's no guessing in a book, especially one you've already read.

After school, Luís is waiting at my locker, and my stomach somersaults faster with each step I take toward him.

"Vanessa says you're mad at me."

"Aren't *you* the one who's mad?"

"No. Why would you think that?"

How can he be so smart in school but clueless about a girl's feelings after she's been ignored? "Because I called to apologize about the dance, but you never called back."

"Well," he admits. "I *was* mad. For a few days. So I ignored the phone when I saw your number on the caller ID."

"Why didn't you call when you weren't angry anymore?"

"Because I went with my family to Mexico."

Suddenly I remembered his mom mentioning their trip at the dance. So that's where he was. I can't believe I forgot he was leaving town.

"Believe me," he continued, "I wanted to call you from there, but my parents wouldn't let me because international calls are too expensive. But I wrote you a letter. Didn't you get it?"

"No."

"Well, the mail takes a long time from Mexico. Maybe you'll get it this week."

There's an awkward moment between us. A bunch of people jostle past.

"So we've been boyfriend and girlfriend this whole time?" I ask.

Luís laughs. "Of course." Then he reaches into his backpack. "I got something for you. A Christmas present. I spent hours looking for the perfect one."

I'm thinking he went shopping, but a boyfriend who wears a sundial on his wrist doesn't buy stuff like jewelry. Instead, he gets his girlfriend a beautiful purple sock with a lavender ribbon tied around the ankle band.

"Sock wrap. Get it?" he says.

And I do. Instead of gift wrap, Luís has used a pretty sock. I untie the ribbon, reach inside, and pull out a whelk, a large shell, creamy beige with light brown spots.

"Listen," he says, putting the shell to my ear so I can hear the echoing of waves and wind. "Remember?"

And I do remember as the sound reminds me of our special moment on the beach when we sat on the log and listened to the stuttering of the sea. Then I realize that something about Luís is different. He stood in front of the whole class and spoke *without stuttering*! I'm *positive* he didn't get stuck on any words. Every now and then, he *almost* stuttered, but he stopped himself, took a deep breath, and talked on.

"You haven't been stuttering," I say.

He pushes up his glasses and smiles a little.

"I've been seeing that speech therapist your dad told me about," he explains.

I punch his shoulder. "Why didn't you tell me?" I say.

"I wanted to surprise you. I wanted to see if you'd notice."

"Of course I'd notice. I notice *everything* about you."

"And your dad helped too. In his own way. While I waited for my appointment, he taught me how to make up these Shakespearean insults. Stuff like puny, dizzy-eyed maggot or vain, swag-bellied lout or slobbering, wart-skinned lizard."

I crack up. "You sound just like him."

"He says if I can handle Shakespearean insults, then I can handle stuff like 'Good morning.' You're lucky to have him for a dad."

"I am?"

"Of course, you slimy, toad-spotted rock."

"Did you just call me a slimy, toad-spotted rock? Those are fighting words, you wimpy, oozy-skinned slug."

"Hey, that's pretty good," Luís laughs. "I didn't know you could do that."

"Maybe my dad never taught me how to pitch a base-ball," I explain, "but he sure did teach me how to pitch a Shakespearean insult."

Confetti Rain

As soon as I see my dad, I hug him.

"Thanks for teaching Luís those Shakespearean insults."

He laughs a little. "They work magic, don't they?"

"Sure do. He did a whole presentation without stuttering."

My dad nods, proud. I can tell he's imagining the scene, but after a moment, he returns to his book. He's reading something called *One Hundred Years of Solitude*.

I wonder if that's how he feels. As if he's been alone for one hundred years.

"It's your fault," I say. "About feeling lonely for a hundred years."

I point at the book cover, and he glances at it.

"You know how you're always telling me that stories are important?" I say.

"They *are* important."

"I know. I never really believed you, but now I'm beginning to understand."

I pause, trying to figure out how to explain myself.

"I have a confession to make," I say. "All this time you've been reading books, I've been writing one."

"Really? What's it about?"

"It's about my life. I write whatever comes to mind. It started out as a joke, but then I got into it. Before I knew it, I was writing a classic epic journey."

"You mean like Luke Skywalker?"

"I mean like the rabbits in *Watership Down.* Sort of. I'm not sure. I can't seem to write the last chapter." I pause a minute. "Would you like to read it?"

"Of course," he says. "Hand it over."

I open my backpack and pull out my version of the Hazel and Fiver adventure. My dad notices the official-looking folder with the APOLONIA FLORES label, but he doesn't ask any questions. He opens it and starts reading. I sit on the couch and wait, watching as he winces, chuckles, or glances at me with lots of worry.

When he finishes, he puts the folder on the end table and says, "I think Hazel's dad needs to come out of the rabbit hole and say something." He leans forward and reaches for my hand. His fingers are warm and firm. "Something like I'm sorry. Like you shouldn't have to go through all this gloom and doom by yourself. You've got your whole life ahead of you." He looks down with a bit of shame on his face.

"Do you know what I wish for?" I say. "I wish . . . I wish you'd get out of your rabbit hole, Dad. I mean . . . how am I supposed to move on when you won't? What happened to Mom is terrible, but . . ." I get stuck for a moment, then I remember what Mrs. Huerta said. "Today I learned that we can't make up for lost time. Once it's gone, it's gone. Like, I won't get to play soccer this year. And I'll never get my Christmas holiday back, so I feel really stupid for wasting it with a bad mood. Soon, it'll be two years since Mom died. Two years of life in a rabbit hole, and I don't think I can take another depressing day. I don't think you can either!"

I start crying. I feel like a tower of cards, made from the hearts and spades of sadness, anger, frustration, and shame — and this last card, this moment of telling Dad that I miss him, that I *need* him, is the one that makes me crash down. Dad holds me, rocks me, and kisses the top of my head. I feel like a baby again, and it embarrasses me. But being comforted feels good too, and soon I'm too exhausted and at peace to cry.

I nod to let Dad know that I feel better now. He goes to the restroom and brings me a box of tissues so I can dry my face. His eyes and cheeks look wet too.

"Remember what Mom used to say?" I ask.

He nods.

"Después de la lluvia sale el sol."

"That's right," he says. "She also liked to say, *el árbol se conoce por su fruta*."

"A tree is known by its fruit?"

"Or, like mother, like daughter. And you are, Lina. You're just as smart and beautiful as your mother."

I blush. I don't think of myself as smart and beautiful, but if Dad says so, then it must be true.

"I've been a terrible father."

"Only when you serve beans from a can without heating them up first," I tease.

He chuckles. So do I.

"Can I ask you a question?" I say.

"Anything."

"Does reading all those books make you feel better?"

"No." He surprises me. "They just help me forget things for a while."

"Things like Mom?"

"No. I could never forget her." He thinks a minute. "If I read a book, then I can be someone else for a while. And even if they're sad, at least they're sad for different reasons."

"But then the book ends," I say.

"That's right. And here I am in this empty house again."

"But, Dad, the house isn't empty. *I'm* here. And we've got two friends across the street who really care about us." I pause to let this sink in. "I know you and Ms. Cantu argued the other night."

"You do?"

I nod. "I've got a confession to make. About something Vanessa and I did. We wanted to help Ms. Cantu, so Vanessa thought it would be a great idea to . . ."

"Are you talking about those silly poems you wrote?"

"You know about that?"

"Of course. Irma figured it out after the first poem. She showed it to me. You really made us laugh with all that Silver Fox stuff."

"The thing is," I try to explain, "you and Ms. Cantu have been so miserable, and after a while, it really wears us down. Vanessa and I just wanted things to be normal again. I know we were wrong about the phony love poems, but maybe Ms. Cantu's right. Maybe you guys *should* date for a while."

"Date? Wherever did you get that idea?"

"From you and Ms. Cantu. Wasn't that why you were arguing?"

He laughs, a deep, belly-jiggling laugh.

"What were you talking about then?" I say, realizing I'd made a mistake. "What did you guys mean about trying things out for a month and the kids being all happy about it?"

"Oh, Lina," he barely manages. "She doesn't want me to be her boyfriend. She wants me to be in the school play. The kids she's talking about are my students."

"That's why you've been ignoring her?"

"She's the most stubborn woman in the world. She's

got the whole school bugging me. I can't teach in peace anymore. Plus, every time I'm with her, she makes me try crazy things, but you know me. I just like to . . ."

"Read," I finish.

"Exactly."

"But you have to admit, Dad, when you and Ms. Cantu are together, you seem really happy."

He thinks for a minute. "You're right," he says. "We have a lot of fun. But then I feel guilty because your mom's not here."

"She wouldn't want that," I say. "She wouldn't want you to be lonely or angry for a hundred years like the people in your book."

"You're right," he says, glancing at my Hazel and Fiver story. "I guess I have to get out of the rabbit hole, don't I?"

We decide to visit our friends, so we cross the street and step through Ms. Cantu's door without even knocking. She's in the kitchen. The vinegar smell is powerful. Ms. Cantu's table has bowls of orange, purple, and green dye. Three or four eggshells are soaking in each bowl while others dry on newspapers. With the pointy tip of Elmer's Glue, she's drawing zigzags and diamonds on the finished *cascarones* and then sprinkling them with glitter. Her whole kitchen's a factory.

"Well, hello, stranger," Ms. Cantu says when she sees my dad.

"I need to tell you something," he says. "I just . . .

you see . . . I want to apologize for ignoring you lately.
It's just . . . it's just . . ."

"Just what?" she asks, impatient.

"Just that you won't take 'no' for an answer."

She stares at him, thinking this over. Then she takes
the *cascarón* in her hand and cracks it on his head — glue,
glitter, everything.

"What's that for?" my dad says, brushing off the confetti and picking at the eggshell stuck in his hair.

"That's for refusing to be in the play."

"What's going on?" Vanessa asks as she comes in
from a back room.

"Your mom wants my dad to be in a play."

"Since when?"

"Since their big fight, remember?"

"You said they were fighting because my mom made
moves on your dad." She grabs a confetti egg and threat-
ens me with it.

"Made moves?" Ms. Cantu says. "What does this
mean?"

"Lina thought you wanted me to be your boyfriend,"
Dad explains.

"That's crazy!" She grabs an egg. "What other ru-
mors have you started, young lady?"

"I wasn't starting a rumor," I say, grabbing my own
cascarón in self-defense. "My imagination got a little wild,
that's all. That's what happens when I'm bored, when my
best friend spends the entire holiday hanging out with her
dad and ignoring me."

"She wasn't hanging out with her dad," Ms. Cantu says. "She was hanging out with his *other* woman and with Carlos, her secret boyfriend."

"Lina! You *told* her? You big tattletale!"

Vanessa cracks the egg on my head, and I fight back by cracking one on hers.

"I *am not* a tattletale!"

"It's true," Ms. Cantu says to Vanessa. "Your *father* told me. Just imagine how I felt when your father made a big deal about how much fun you had at the spa with that woman and about how nice he is for letting you see your boyfriend since I won't."

"Well, I have to sneak around," Vanessa says. "You're such a man-hater." She grabs another egg. "This is for hating Dad all the time."

She cracks it on Ms. Cantu's head.

"Don't be mad at *me*," Ms. Cantu tells her, "after your dad acted cruel and selfish. Although . . ."

Just then, Ms. Cantu gets assaulted by another *cascarón,* this one from my dad.

"Why did you do that?" she asks.

"Because. I'm a big, cruel, selfish man."

Vanessa laughs, "Way to go, Mr. Flores. That's teaching her a lesson."

"I already learned my lesson," Ms. Cantu says. "It's true. The divorce really hurt me. But since my accident, Homero's been helping out, plus the custodians at school. And the mailman brings my letters and newspaper to the door, so I won't have to walk to the curb. Some men are jerks, but most are really nice." Ms. Cantu grabs another egg. "Now it's payback time," she says. "For jumping to conclusions about me."

I don't know if the payback's for Vanessa or my dad or me because suddenly we're having a *cascarones* war. I crack eggs on Dad, on Vanessa, on Ms. Cantu. They crack eggs on me and on each other. We don't care what stage the *cascarones* are in. We grab finished ones and half-finished ones; eggs stuffed with confetti and eggs waiting to be stuffed. Even with one leg in a cast, Ms. Cantu can move. We run around the kitchen bumping into things and tripping over ourselves. Soon streaks of confetti color the air like silent fireworks.

The whole time, we accuse each other.

"You messed up my whooping crane project!"

"You messed up your English grade!"

"You make it impossible for me to have boyfriends!"

"You have boyfriends behind my back!"

We go on and on. Finally my dad grabs two eggs and cracks them on his own head. He looks so silly. He makes us laugh till we cry — a happy cry — a cry to squeeze out the last tears, the last bit of blame.

Then, he cracks a third one, and as he shakes off the confetti, he says, "That's for spending more time with my books than with my daughter," then, looking at Vanessa and Ms. Cantu, "and with my friends."

I follow his example. "This is for sending those silly poems," I say, cracking the first *cascarón,* "and for failing English," cracking the second, "and for jumping to conclusions and holding grudges all the time." That, I believe, deserves two confetti eggs.

"These," Ms. Cantu says, holding *cascarones* in both hands, "are for thinking all men are jerks." She sandwiches her head with them, laughing the whole time.

"This is for ignoring Lina," Vanessa says. "And these are for all the lies I told my mom." She cracks one, two, three, four, five *cascarones*. "I told a lot of lies," she laughs, grabbing a fresh carton.

"Here, let me help you get rid of your lies," I say.

And before I know it, we're back to running around and cracking confetti eggs on each other's heads. But this time, our *cascarones* war is really a *cascarones* celebration.

"Let's break them all!" my dad says.

And we do, crushing the *cascarones* in our hands and throwing up the confetti, then watching the confetti rain down as colorful and free as our joy.

GLOSSARY OF *DICHOS*

Los amigos mejores son libros –
Books are your best friends

El gato dormido no caza ratón –
The sleeping cat doesn't catch the rat

Una acción buena enseña más que mil palabras –
Actions speak louder than words

Un amigo es el mejor espejo –
A friend is the best mirror

Querer es poder –
To desire is to be able to do

Buñolero, ¡haz tus buñuelos! –
*Buñuelo maker, make your buñuelos: in other
words, mind your own business!*

Quien bien te quiere te hará llorar –
Those who love you the most will make you cry

En boca cerrada no entran moscas –
Flies can't enter a closed mouth

Dime con quién andas y te dire quién eres –
*Tell me who you hang out with and I'll tell you who
you are*

Lo mismo el chile que aguja, a todos pican igual –
Both the chile and the needle sting

No preguntes lo que no te importa –
Don't ask about things that aren't your concern

Las mentiras no tienen pies –
*Lies don't have feet so they can't travel on
their own*

El camarón que se duerme se lo lleva la corriente –
*The shrimp that goes to sleep gets carried away by
the current*

Después de la lluvia sale el sol –
After the rain, the sun shines

No tengas como vano el consejo del anciano –
Don't ignore advice from someone with experience

Más vale solo que mal acompañado –
It's better to be alone than in bad company

Cada cabeza es un mundo –
Inside each head lies a different world

El silencio es oro –
Silence is golden

Para el gato viejo, ratón tierno –
A tender mouse for an old cat

Panza llena, corazón contento –
Full belly, happy heart

Perro que no camina no encuentra hueso –
The dog that doesn't walk doesn't find the bone

La educación es la única cosa que
nadie te podrá quitar –
An education is the only thing that
can't be taken away

El mal escribano le echa la culpa a la pluma –
A poor writer blames the pen

Del dicho al hecho hay gran trecho –
It's a long way from saying you're going to do
something to actually doing it

Hasta el diablo una vez fue ángel –
Even the devil was once an angel

Donde hay gana, hay maña –
Where there is desire, there is ability

La mejor palabra es la que no se dice –
The best word is the one that is not spoken

Caras vemos, corazones no sabemos –
We can see people's faces but not their hearts

Lo que bien se aprende, nunca se pierde –
What is well learned is never lost

El árbol se conoce por su fruta –
A tree is known by its fruit

Acknowledgments

I'd like to thank the Alfredo Cisneros del Moral Foundation for giving me and my fellow Texas writers an opportunity to tell our stories. A big thank you to Stefanie Von Borstel, Alvina Ling, and Connie Hsu for wonderful suggestions and for fighting to get this book out there. Also, my Daedalus friends — Irma Ned Bailey, Cindy Leal Massey, Linda Shuler, Bill Stephens, and Florence Weinberg — you guys keep me writing. Finally, thanks to all those who put up with me. My friends — Vanesa, Kirk, Rick, Caryl, and San Juan; my family — Mom, Dad, Albert, Tricia, Steven, *y mis sobrinos*; and Gene, both family *and* friend.